Plains' Wolf

The honest folk of Bedrock had watched the lone rider on the edge of the plains' town with much the same suspicion as they would a prowling wolf. It seemed as though that was as close as they and Sheriff Sam Berrins were ever going to get until, for no good reason that anyone could fathom, the worst and meanest of the territory's gunslingers began to gather in town.

Their arrival and the disappearance of banker Newton Carfax were to spark a bitter struggle for survival where a Colt blazed on every corner and even the shadows seemed to bleed. But the trouble really started when the plains' wolf broke his cover and began to howl....

By the same author

Rain Guns
Hennigan's Reach
Hennigan's Law
Shadow Hand
Bloodline
The Oldster
Border Kill
Bitter Sands
Go Hang the Man
Gun Loose
Drift Raiders
Trail Breaker
Shoot to Live

Plains' Wolf

DAN CLAYMAKER

A Black Horse Western

ROBERT HALE · LONDON

© Dan Claymaker 2001
First published in Great Britain 2001

ISBN 0 7090 6873 5

Robert Hale Limited
Clerkenwell House
Clerkenwell Green
London EC1R 0HT

The right of Dan Claymaker
to be identified as author of this work has been
asserted by him in accordance with the Copyright,
Designs and Patents Act 1988.

Typeset by
Derek Doyle & Associates, Liverpool.
Printed and bound in Great Britain by
Antony Rowe Limited, Wiltshire

*This one for T and S
when they finally hit the trail*

ONE

The big blow late summer winds off the Seroquoi plains were a bad omen as far as the folk of Bedrock were concerned. No good ever came of them. First drift of a dust cloud and you could smell the mood of the winter coming up; or so they reckoned. Others of a more circumspect nature would figure for the swirling dirt hiding a whole heap of trouble. Either way the blow was never welcome. And that year the summer had been poor and the winds arrived early. . . .

Sheriff Sam Berrins wiped the dirt from his face, turned his back on the wind and reined his mount to the grey huddled buildings of the town.

No point in wasting any more time chasing ghosts, he thought, pulling the collar of his coat into his neck. Whoever it was had been out here had seen all he wanted and moved on. Hardly blame him for that; not a deal to recommend Bedrock in any weather, least of all at the start of the blow. Fellow had an ounce of sense he would put the Seroquoi plains firmly behind him and head west for the prospect of an easy winter and an early spring.

Even so, something about the town had intrigued the man. Something important enough to keep him here on the windswept plains for three whole days. Something he had been looking for, waiting on, expecting to see, watching for, always at the same distance, same steady pace in a slow circling drift until he must have known every plank and nail, door and window of the rear of every town building as well as he knew the back of his own hand.

Just that, for three days – lone rider and horse, harsh in the brighter light, blurred and faded when the wind swirled the dirt and the dust clouds shimmered.

Storekeeper Henry Clarke had been among the first to draw Sam's attention to the presence.

'Don't make no sense no how, does it?' he had frowned, tidying his counter for the second time in as many minutes. 'What's the fella want with just sittin' out there, starin' like he was seein' a ghost? Why don't he ride in, come right out with it, say what he wants, ask all he needs? Save a whole lot of bother, if yuh ask me. Spooky, I call it.'

'And you can say that again, Henry Clarke,' the mayor's wife, Amelia Carfax, had huffed, emerging from behind a mound of blankets. 'It isn't natural. Said as much to the mayor only last night. Why, I said, who's to say the man isn't sick, or something? We wouldn't know, would we? Perhaps we should ask Doc Peppers to go take a look.'

'Fella's got a tongue in his head whoever he is, ain't he?' Charlie Formes had growled from his seat at the store's open door. 'He don't talk, there ain't nobody listenin'. Common sense.'

'Well, I don't know,' Henry had begun again with another flourish of the duster across the counter. 'All very well sayin' he's got a tongue in his head—'

'Yuh sayin' he ain't?' Charlie had snapped.

'No, o'course I ain't. All I'm sayin' is—'

'What do you think, Sheriff?' the woman had interrupted brusquely. 'Have you given any thought to the matter?'

Sam Berrins had given no thought whatsoever to the matter, much less bothered to seek out the man. 'Well, no, ma'am, can't say I've given it *that* much thought, but like yuh say—'

'Yuh should mebbe go take a good long look, eh? Get out there, mebbe talk to the fella,' Henry had urged. 'Heck, he goes on like this and we'll none of us be sleepin' easy in our beds. I mean, where's he gettin' his food and water? Where's he beddin' down – if he is – and just supposin—'

'Yes, yes, I think we hear what you're saying, Mr Clarke,' the woman had said dismissively. 'And I'm equally sure the sheriff understands his responsibilities.' She had flounced importantly to the door. 'I shall tell the mayor you are looking into the situation,' she had added with, a gratuitous smile and fluttering of eyelashes.

Sam Berrins had merely tipped his hat and grunted.

*

But a whole morning spent trailing the plains in search of the stranger had revealed nothing, save some evidence in the few dips and hollowed drifts of where the man had slept. Otherwise, Sheriff Berrins had concluded, nothing: after three days of watching, circling, waiting, the fellow had ridden on and left the Seroquoi plains and the town of Bedrock to the late summer winds.

The man's appearance and presence had been a mystery; his departure equally so, and that was how it might have stayed, but for an unseen, unknown, overnight visitor to Henry Clarke's main street store.

'Saw it soon as I set foot in the place to open up,' Henry explained while Sheriff Berrins slipped out of his heavy coat and poured himself a coffee from the pot simmering on his office stove. 'No doubt about it. Back door had been forced sometime last night; mebbe early hours of the mornin'. Plain as the nose on my face. Come and see for y'self.'

'Somebody broke into the store – and took what precisely?' asked Sam, sipping the hot coffee.

'Nothin'! Didn't take a damned thing. I checked and double-checked. Everythin's just as I left it when I locked up.'

Sam crossed slowly, silently to the window and peered into the dust-blown street. 'Yuh tellin' me as how somebody went to all the trouble and took all the risks of breakin' into your store, and took nothin'?' he said quietly.

'That's it, Sam. Didn't take a thing, but he sure as hell left somethin'. S'right. He left this: sheet of paper, one word scrawled across it. Pinned to the counter. Here.'

Sam took the sheet and read aloud the name: 'Shard'.

'Know somethin',' said Henry, 'I figure for that fella who's been watchin' out there on the plain bein' the one as broke in. What he's written there must be his name. Sorta callin' card like them fancy salesmen from back East hand out. I seen plenty of them. Now what in the name of tarnation would he wanna do that for?'

Sheriff Sam Berrins had not the remotest notion, but he was chillingly aware in the sudden howl of the wind that he and the folk of Bedrock had seen nothing like the last of the mysterious plains' rider.

TWO

It took only an hour following Henry Clarke's revelations of the break-in at the store for the news to travel fast, and suitably embellished, through the town and for local banker and mayor, Newton Carfax, to call a meeting of the civic committee in the back room of the Long Spur Saloon.

'Am I reading this right, Sam?' he had begun, helping himself from a newly opened bottle of whiskey. 'You're tellin' me it's a fact that the drifter we had wastin' his good time ridin' round town to no good purpose, left his name on a sheet of paper in Henry's store and went to all the trouble of breakin' in to do so? That what I'm bein' told?'

'That's it,' murmured Sheriff Berrins.

'Straight up,' Henry Clarke nodded. 'That's how it was.'

'Don't make no sense,' grunted Casey Pike, the town blacksmith. 'Yuh ask me, the fella was plumb out of his mind. Crazy. The sorta thing crazy folk get to doin'. Ain't that so, Doc?'

Doc Peppers examined the glowing bowl of his pipe for a moment before answering. 'Crazy folk can do all manner of things, but doin' what the stranger did, when he did it and the manner of the doin', don't make him crazy. He mebbe had good reason for leavin' his name. He's mebbe as sane as any one of us here.'

The mayor gulped his drink and pushed the bottle across the table to the blacksmith. 'You ever heard of a fella by the name of Shard?' he asked, turning again to the sheriff. 'He wanted or anythin' like that?

'Nothin' on the sheets, and I ain't never heard of nobody by that name,' replied Sam.

A cloud of cigar smoke drifted to the ceiling as saloon owner, Lawson Ridges, cleared his throat and blew specks of ash from his shirt front. 'What's it matter, anyhow?' he said, eyeing the assembly as if about to deliver a sermon. 'Who's botherin'? I ain't. Fella turns up, prowls round town like a hungry wolf for three whole days, don't fetch up in the street, or anywhere else come to that, and rides out.'

'Not before breakin' into my store,' piped Henry indignantly.

'So what?' shrugged Ridges behind another cloud of smoke. 'Didn't take nothin', did he? Left yuh with a sheet of paper and a busted door. No big deal, is it? Probably broke into your place because it was closest – or mebbe the easiest.'

'What yuh suggestin' there?' blustered Henry.

'All right,' snapped Carfax, 'we ain't here for snipin' at each other.'

'We ain't here for no good reason I can see,'

drawled the blacksmith. 'Fella's gone and chances are we'll never see hide or hair of him again. Leavin' his name don't mean a thing. Like I say, just crazy.' He rubbed his chin. 'Yuh want that back door fixed, Henry, I'll do it for nothin'.'

Henry grunted and poured a measure from the bottle. 'Well, mebbe you're right at that,' he said, taking the glass in his hand. 'Mebbe it don't count for much. And, sure, doubt if we will ever see Mr Shard, or whoever he is, again. Best we can do is just ask for Sam here to keep a watch for him.'

The sheriff grunted, the blacksmith smiled and Lawson Ridges blew a long spiral of smoke.

'So that'll be the way of it,' said Carfax, adjusting his expansive cravat. 'No cause for alarm, we simply—'

' 'Course,' said Doc Peppers quietly, tamping the bowl of his pipe, 'there is another aspect of the matter we seem to have overlooked.' He paused, raising his soft grey eyes in a thoughtful stare. 'We don't know the fella's name is Shard, do we? Supposin' it ain't. What then? And supposin' it's like Lawson there says: supposin' he was a hungry wolf on the prowl. . . .

'Hungry for what?'

Sheriff Sam Berrins had figured on taking Doc Peppers aside later that night to probe deeper into the doubt surrounding the stranger he had planted in the minds of the town committee.

His deputy, Frank Baker, however, had presented a more pressing problem.

'Best get ourselves down to the Long Spur, Sam.' he had warned, buckling his gun belt to his favoured high reach. 'I hear we got trouble brewin'. Some unsavoury lookin' – and smellin' – character name of Dyke rode in off the plains' trail at sundown. Peaceable enough 'til he hit the bottle and turned his unwelcome attentions on the girls. Mr Ridges says as how we should—'

'I hear yuh, Frank,' sighed Sam, reaching to the gun cabinet for his Winchester. 'Duty calls, and when duty calls—'

'Lawmen walk!' smiled Baker.

'Yuh got it. Let's walk!'

It had been the whipping howl and bone-searching chill of the big blow winds that had driven Scully Dyke in search of the comforts of a bed and whoever he could cajole into sharing it with him for the night.

Arriving one day late at his planned destination of the northern stage town of Asparity was hardly going to count. And meanwhile, Bedrock was huddled right there two miles off the main trail and looking, even in this dust-swirling weather, as tempting as a creek stream to a parched man.

Bedrock it would be, he had decided late that afternoon and, in so doing, sealed his fate the minute he had turned his back on the Seroquoi plains' wind. . . .

The wind was still whipping and howling, fingering every last loose clapboard in the street, snapping and snarling at anything not tied down, swinging the saloon batwings to a rhythmic squeak and creak as Sheriff Berrins and his deputy stepped to the boardwalk fronting them and paused to listen to the raised voice commanding the bar.

'Now I ain't one for makin' a big meal of words,' Dyke was attempting to say without losing his way in the drunken slurs, 'so we'll make this kinda quick, eh, and get it done with. That way we all stay happy.' He belched loudly. 'Fact is – fact, I say – this young lady here, Sadie by name, so I gather, is mine. Yuh hear that? Mine.'

'Sadie might have somethin' to say about that, mister,' came a voice from somewhere in a shadowed corner.

Dyke swayed, belched again, peered dazedly across the gloom and pulled the girl tighter to his side. 'Well, now, fella, whoever yuh are, she might at that, but not on your orderin' she won't. So if you'd care to step out where I can see yuh—'

'You lookin' for a fight, mister?' called another voice. ' 'Cus if yuh are, yuh should be knowin' we don't fight drunks, not in this town we don't. Fella's gotta be standin' straight if he wants to fight.'

'Yuh bet – and he ain't got to be clingin' to no piece of skirt neither!' quipped the man's partner.

Dyke's bloodshot eyes rolled in his head. A glistening of sweat lathered his brow, trickling in thin lines to merge with the trail dirt on his stubbled cheeks. He growled and pushed the girl aside. 'Oh, my. Oh, my, if that ain't the sorta talk comes like music to my ears. Yessir! You ease clear of that table there, fella, and I'll show yuh who's standin' straight, and show the rest of yuh how fast I can stiffen out a fella. Now shift, damn yuh!'

'Time we moved,' murmured the sheriff to his deputy. 'Yuh see anythin' of Ridges?'

'Waitin', watchin', top of the stairs,' said Frank Baker.

Sam grunted, eased the Winchester into his hip and pushed the 'wings open on a high-pitched squeak. 'That'll be far enough, mister,' he ordered, levelling the rifle. 'Just cut that gunbelt loose and step away. We don't want no trouble, and you can bet we ain't havin' any. You hear me, fella?'

Dyke's glazed eyes, narrowed. The sweat thickened and glistened. His gun hand hovered like a moth above the butt of his holstered Colt.

'Just do it, mister,' ordered Sam again.

'Go to hell, Lawman,' growled Dyke, the Colt bristling in his grip at almost the same moment he threw himself to one side, the blaze of his shot ripping the silence to shreds.

Sam's Winchester roared, but the aim was high and Dyke already falling clear of it. Only then as Sam levelled again did he hear the groan, the sudden gasps, the crash of a table behind him.

'He's hit Frank, damnit!' somebody shouted.

Sam released his shot, straight as a shaft of light into Scully Dyke's arm, spinning the Colt from his grip.

'He's dead – Frank's dead!'

Sam spun round to the sprawled, bleeding body of his deputy, then spun again to face Dyke, sunk to his knees, his fingers crimson in the flow of blood from his wound.

The bar drinkers waited open-mouthed and wide-eyed for what they were certain would be another roar from the Winchester. But all they heard was Sam Berrins's voice.

'On yuh feet, rat. Take a short walk to Hell!'

THREE

'Pity – he's goin' to live!' Doc Peppers slammed shut the door to the cell, turned the key and returned it to the sheriff's desk. 'Could've saved yourself a whole lot of trouble there, Sam, if yuh'd just shot the sonofabitch back at the Spur.'

He crossed the office to the table in the corner, washed his hands in the bowl of freshly poured water, picked up a towel and came to Sam Berrins's side at the night darkened window. 'A bad business. I'm sorry.' He dried his hands carefully in the towel, his gaze flitting quickly to the sheriff's taut, impassive face. 'Yuh can wake the scumbag there whenever you've a mind. What yuh plannin'? Standin' him to trial?' Doc grunted and flourished the towel indignantly. 'He worth the bother?'

'Frank Baker would've reckoned on the law takin' its course,' murmured Sam. 'I owe the trial and hangin' to Frank. Wouldn't see it other.'

'I'll swear yuh shot him tryin' to escape if yuh want to finish the rat now.'

'He'll hang, Doc. Let him sweat on the prospect.'

Doc sighed. 'Suit yourself. You're the man with the badge. Yuh goin' to trail him out to Marshal Renwick at Asparity?'

'Soon as it's light and the wind eases a mite. Circuit judge is due there in three days.'

Doc laid aside the towel. 'Yuh want me to ride with yuh? No problem if you do.'

'I'll manage fine, Doc, but thanks all the same.' Sam turned to gaze at the man sprawled in a sweating sleep on the cell bed. 'Don't reckon for him troublin' me none, look of that wound he's carryin'.'

'Painful,' winced Doc, behind a wry smile. 'And I ain't exactly made it any easier! Wound's clean and bandaged, and that's as good as it'll get.' He slipped into his frock coat and settled his hat on his head. 'Best get over to the Spur. See if Sadie and the girls need any lookin' to.'

'Thanks again,' murmured Sam.

Doc Peppers shrugged, collected his bag, glanced at the cell and had reached the door to the street when he paused, his hand still on the latch. 'Seroquoi winds are early this year. Yuh noticed? And they don't smell good, Sam. Nossir, they do not. So you watch yourself, eh? Don't take no chances.' He opened the door. 'See yuh around.'

Sam watched the dark, stooped figure of Doc Peppers disappearing into the shadows of the wind-whipped street. Maybe he should have got to asking him about the stranger, about who he might, or might not, have been. But maybe not – not on this night, with Frank Baker stiffening back there at the funeral parlour.

He drew his Colt slowly from its holster, weighed and balanced it in his grip, tightened his hold as he turned and crossed the office to the cell.

He took careful aim on a spot plumb between the eyes of the sleeping man. Easy. One shot. Perhaps a groan, a twist, and he would be dead. Cold as Frank Baker come sun-up.

Sonofa-goddamn-bitch!

Sam clanged the barrel of the gun across the cell bars until Scully Dyke's eyes sprang open as if staring into a nightmare and the sweat swamped his vision.

'The big blow here early; ghosts sitting out there on the plain, some crazed gunslinger shootin' up the bar and killin' a deputy lawman.... I tell yuh, Lawson, the future ain't lookin' one bit bright from where I'm standin'.' Newton Carfax tossed a measure of whiskey to the back of his throat. 'So what we goin' to do about it?'

'What are *we* goin' to do about it?' smiled Lawson Ridges, relaxing in the plush expanse of an easy chair in his private quarters at the saloon. "Are *we* supposed to do anythin' about it? And what is it you want to do somethin' about? Sheriff's taken care of the shootin'. That Dyke fella's sweatin' it out in a cell, and Sam'll ride him out to a trial and hangin' at Asparity soon as he can. Simple as that.'

'And that fella we had watchin' the town – what about him? Said yourself as how he was prowlin' like some wolf. And what about Doc's opinion? Damnit, we might—'

'Hold it,' said Ridges, raising an arm. 'You're frettin' there worse than that gossipin' wife of yours! Steady up, will yuh? Fella who left the note at the store has pulled out, and that's the end of it. We shan't be seein' no more of him. Crazy as a coot. As for Doc Peppers – Doc sees the worst in everythin'. Way of life, ain't it? Spends too much time watchin' folk die. T'ain't healthy.'

'That's easy enough to say, but what about—?'

'Why don't yuh pour yourself another drink, Mr Mayor, and relax? Or is it all that money you're sittin' on at your bank out there that's botherin' yuh? That's mebbe closer to the truth of it, eh?'

'Well,' began Carfax, circling through the soft glow of the lantern-lit room, 'I gotta admit we are carryin' a mite more cash than usual since you and me sold out on them railroad bonds last month, and I get twitchy when money's just sittin' there. Be another month at least before we dare start transferrin' sums to Asparity, and only then—'

'So there you are, that's your problem,' grinned Ridges, coming quickly to his feet. 'T'ain't the weather, prowlin' riders or even gut-rotten gunslingers troublin' yuh: it's money. A small fortune, as it happens, and not one dollar of it acquired legally. Right?'

'No need to say it quite so loud,' said Carfax, glancing nervously into the shadows.

'Hell, Newton, ain't nobody here but the two of us. Relax, pour yourself that drink, and then I'll go get one of the girls to keep yuh company. I take it yuh ain't goin' home to yuh wife yet awhile?'

'Well, I mebbe should,' murmured the mayor.

'But yuh ain't,' soothed Ridges, laying an arm across the man's shoulders. 'Let's have a drink and get to talkin' some more about how we're going to spend all that money we got stashed away. Now ain't that one helluva future to look to? Don't come no brighter.'

Newton Carfax's smile was frail and fitful, as if twisted on a sudden whip of the plains' wind.

Henry Clarke cursed, pulled on his pants, flicked the braces to his shoulders and took the lantern firmly in his grip. Damnit, he thought, stepping carefully through the shadowy half gloom of the store, this was no time of night to be padding about like some arthritic old mouse.

He should have fixed that shack door out back weeks ago; should have known the big blow winds would get to it sooner or later. And now they had, with all the vengeance of a devil unleashed. Be clean off its hinges before midnight at this rate.

He stepped out to the cluttered rear of the store, heaved the door shut behind him, caught his breath in a gasp against the buffeting wind and swirling clouds of dirt, and struggled to the shack, the lantern swinging wildly in his grip.

'Hell let loose!' he groaned, putting his weight to the creaking shack door, its top hinge already broken clear of the jamb. 'Of all the. . . .'

It was then, in the sudden dance of flickering

lantern light, that he saw it: a sack of beans, slashed at one corner, the contents spilled and gathering to heaps in the rush of the wind.

'What the devil. . . .'

But Henry's words were lost on the gusts and the realization that it was not so much the plains' wind that had loosened the shack door as the efforts of somebody breaking in; somebody who had cut open the sack and helped himself.

And very recently. Henry had checked his stocks at noon that day and all had been in order.

The wolf was still on the prowl, he thought, staring at the scattered beans. And getting hungry.

FOUR

'Yuh sure he didn't leave another note? Yuh've checked?' Doc Peppers adjusted his spidery armed spectacles and peered intently over them.

'I've checked. Every darned inch of the place, soon as it was full light. He didn't leave no note. Just helped himself to the beans.' Henry Clarke turned his hat nervously through his hands as he crossed to the window of the parlour and stared into the empty street. 'Spooky, ain't it?'

'Well, proves one thing for certain,' said Doc, smoothing his waistcoat over his paunch, 'the fella ain't done with us yet.'

'But where is he now?' croaked Henry. 'Out there on the plains? Here in town? Some place else? We don't know and there ain't no means of knowin'. And just what in the name of tomorrow does he want with a town like Bedrock?' Henry swung round, his face gaunt and pale. 'What we got that almost any other town's got double of? We ain't nobody, and there ain't nothin' to hide.'

'Ah,' said Doc, adjusting his spectacles, 'now there you might be wrong, Henry Clarke. Mebbe Bedrock has got somethin' to hide. Or somebody.'

'What yuh sayin'?' frowned Henry.

'Just that,' shrugged Doc. 'Could be there is somethin' here that somebody don't want known.'

'Not to my knowledge.' The storekeeper stiffened importantly. 'Ain't much escapes me back there at the store. I hear most things. And I get to seein' more than most. No, if somebody was hidin' somethin', I'd know.'

Doc shrugged again. 'I'll take your word for it, Henry,' he said, with a slow, careful smile. 'Meantime, I suggest we keep this latest development to ourselves, eh? Sam Berrins trailed out for Asparity with that fella Dyke roped behind him at crack of dawn, and yuh know how jumpy Carfax can be; as for Ridges and Casey. . . . Well now, do we need to bother the whole committee with this? I think not.'

Henry murmured something inaudible and fidgeted the hat through his fingers.

'I reckon for the pair of us keepin' a watch on things, leastways 'til Sam gets back. If this fella Shard, or whoever he is, puts in another appearance, we don't want the whole town frettin' on it, do we? Might scare the fella off.'

'Ain't that precisely what we want?'

'Not necessarily so,' said Doc quietly. 'It might be a whole sight more in our interests to find out just what it is the fella wants – or who he wants.' Doc tapped a finger against the side of his nose. 'We should keep watchin', Henry. You and me.'

Henry winked knowingly. 'I'll get back to the store,' he whispered. 'Just in case.'

'You do that, old friend,' said Doc, ushering Henry to the door. 'And if yuh see or hear anythin' . . . yuh know where I am.'

Doc waited until Henry Clarke was deep into the street on his way to the store before turning from the window and crossing to his desk in the far corner of the room. He opened the middle drawer and took the faded, yellowing pages of the newspaper carefully into his hands before spreading them across the desktop.

He pushed his spectacles tight againt the bridge of his nose and leaned closer.

This edition of the *Mid-West Clarion* was more than a year old, but the print was clear enough and there was no doubting the headline in the centre column of page two:

NOTORIOUS
GUNMAN
GOES FREE

Lucas Shard
Released
from County
Penitentiary

*

Sam Berrins spat the gritty plains' dust from between his teeth, reined his mount to a halt and turned his narrowed gaze to the man seated on the tow-roped horse at his back.

Scully Dyke looked about as miserable as the cloud-heavy, wind-chilled day, his body slumped in the saddle, legs loose, head lolling and rolling to the uncertain momentum, the pain from his shoulder wound numbed to a dead weight one minute, throbbing and stabbed through with hot pokers the next.

But he would make it, thought Sam, spitting more dust as he pulled his coat collar high into his neck. 'You bet,' he mouthed, 'all the way to a hanging day!'

He tugged the rope to stir Dyke's attention. 'You'll get all the time yuh need for sleepin' when we hit Asparity,' he called. 'Fact, yuh got the longest sleep of all comin' up!'

Dyke shrugged, raised his head and glared like a caged animal. It was a while before he too spat the dust from his mouth. 'Seroquoi Plains ain't one bit friendly this time of year,' grinned Sam, catching his balance against a squalling gust of wind. 'Suits the occasion, don't it? Fittin'. Sorta chill you'll feel right through yuh bones just before they march yuh out to the noose.'

'Don't get smart, Berrins,' growled the man. 'We ain't there yet, and I still got friends, yuh know.'

'I'm surprised,' mocked Sam. 'Wouldn't have figured for anybody seekin' your company – save for the rats!'

Dyke sneered and spat again. 'We goin' to sit here all day?'

'Gettin' the fidgets? Whole heap of them to come, Scully. Oh, yes, days of 'em, and nights when they just ain't goin' to let yuh sleep. Yuh got plenty to look forward to!'

Sam turned, tightened the tow-rope and walked his mount on into the bite of the swirling wind and the flat grey light of the gloomy day. 'So what ill wind threw yuh up in Bedrock?' he called.

'That any of your business?' snapped Dyke.

'Every lousy thing about you is my business when yuh get to shootin' my deputy.' Sam grated the dirt between his teeth and blinked his wind-sore eyes. 'Yuh should've kept right on ridin', mister.'

'I been kept "right on ridin'" all my life,' sneered Dyke. 'And I ain't done yet!'

Sam smiled quietly to himself. 'You keep dreamin', Scully. I ain't for hurryin' in the nightmares. They'll come soon enough.' He was silent a moment before adding carefully, 'Didn't happen to be meetin' somebody, did yuh?'

Sam felt the rope tighten a mite as the trail mount's pace was checked. He heard Dyke hawk and spit.

'What's it to yuh?' drawled the gunslinger.

'Oh, nothin' of note,' shrugged Sam, his gaze tight, narrowed and fixed ahead. 'Just wonderin' on the sorta vermin you're associatin' with. Call it professional interest.'

'You just reckon yourself lucky I didn't take yuh head off back there,' growled Dyke. 'It just happened to be your day.'

'But not yours, Scully. Nossir. None of yuh scum friends standin' to yuh then, was there? Still, I guess back-shootin' is more their style, eh? Catchin' a fella when he's walkin' away.' Sam tensed, waiting now for the man to snap on the bait of derision.

'I ain't never back-shot a man,' flared Dyke. 'T'ain't my style. I play by the rules. Always have.'

'I'm sure yuh do, but I'd still sure as hell like to know how yuh fetched up in my town, in a place like Bedrock. That don't seem your style neither.'

'On my way to Asparity, weren't I? I got friends up ahead. Sure I have. Who knows, yuh might get to meetin' some of 'em.'

'Well, now, that would be truly somethin',' replied Sam lightly. 'Anybody I'd know?' He licked anxiously at a sudden trickle of sweat.

'Cal Cartwright. Yuh heard of him?'

'I heard. Small time, ain't he?'

'Bob Simmins. Ain't nothin' small time about Bob.'

'Eyesight ain't all it might be these days. And I never rated that low-slung draw of his. Almost as loose as yours, Scully.'

Dyke hawked and spat again as the wind whipped and the dust gathered in a swirl. 'What's with you, Lawman? Got a high opinion of yourself, ain't yuh? Well, mebbe yuh ain't crossed the real guns yet. Mebbe yuh got the likes of Lucas Shard waitin' on yuh.'

Sam's fingers tightened on the reins and the rope to the trail mount. He licked at more sweat, and blinked. 'Shard?' he quizzed, his mind spinning back to the image of the name scrawled on the note left in Henry Clarke's store. 'Do I know him?'

'Released from the Pen at Kee Mounts a year back.'

Sam swallowed the gritty dirt. 'He's here?' he

asked, slowing the pace of his mount. 'You were on your way to a meetin' in Asparity with Lueas Shard?'

Scully Dyke's mouth had opened, the words begun to form, but the only sound ever to clear his throat on that wind-strafed morning on the Seroquoi Plains was a choking, gurgling groan behind the soaring whine of a Winchester's blaze.

FIVE

The shot had come from somewhere far to the left, between a scattering of boulders, a rough outcrop and the softest lift of the plain to a gentle bluff. And might just as well have come from the scudding clouds for all the chance there was of pinpointing it, thought Sam grimly, as he squatted at the lifeless, blood-splattered body of Scully Dyke.

'Hell,' he mouthed, his gaze still tight and narrowed against the wind in its long, sweeping scan of the empty plain where nothing moved save whatever fell prey to the whipping blow. Whoever had been behind the shot would either sit it out in his cover, or had already ridden on. One step too close and Sam might be the next to be biting the plains' dirt.

He grunted, stared at the grimaced, stubble-blackened face of Dyke and pondered on just who had been anxious enough and patient enough to wait for this moment to put an end to the gunslinger. Only one name sprang to mind: Shard.

He grunted again, came fully upright and gazed round him. If Dyke had been on his way to a meeting with Shard somewhere between Bedrock and Asparity, what had they been planning that was so important Dyke had to die with the knowledge still in his head?

Damn it, thought Sam, another few minutes and Dyke might even have got to spitting out the details.

Question now was, if Lucas Shard was recruiting guns, how many was he planning on, who or what was the target, when and where? Might the place be Bedrock? Was Shard the prowling wolf?

But, damn it, why tell the whole town in the note he left? Made no sense.

'Hell,' mouthed Sam again, shifting his gaze back reluctantly to the body of Dyke. Nothing else for it, he decided. He would load the scumbag on the trail mount and return to Bedrock.

It was there, in his own town and the burial in the plain hole they would dig on Boot Hill for Scully Dyke, that the answers to his questions would be found. Twenty minutes later, Sheriff Sam Berrins was loaded up and turning into the whipping bite of the wind.

Leaving one hell for another, he reflected.

Amelia Carfax had been through her husband's pockets twice and still found nothing to confirm her worst fears.

If, as she had long suspected, he was carrying on with one - or maybe more than one - of those cheap, scent-sodden bar girls back at the Long Spur, he was making a good job of covering it up. Doubtless with the connivance of that slippery-sided proprietor, Lawson Ridges, to whom she would not give a place on her porch much less in her parlour.

She replaced the jacket carefully, closing the wardrobe doors with all the stealth of a whispering ghost, waited a moment to be quite certain that her husband was still sleeping soundly, then tiptoed to the bedroom door, stepped to the landing and had the door closed again without so much as the creak of a board or squeak of a hinge.

She waited again, listening to the slow, contented rumble of snoring, smiled softly to herself and hurried on to the stairs.

Nothing to confirm infidelities, she thought, reaching the window in the plushly furnished front parlour, but there had been the key. Not one of his regular keys; not among the bunch on the ring - she knew every one of those, and their purpose, well enough - no, this key had been loose in an inside pocket.

Not at all like Newton to keep a single key loose and apart from the others. He was normally so particular and meticulous, especially where keys were concerned. Keys were security, and security was at the very heart of sound banking. He had said it often enough, almost to the point of boredom – which, when she came to ponder it, suggested one of two possibilities in explanation of the lone key.

It could be that it was something to do with the bank; some new security; a key cut to some recently introduced aspect of the business. But unlikely, she thought. She knew of nothing new at the bank, certainly not requiring the cutting of a special key. And, in any case, a bank key would be with the others on the ring.

So, she considered, pursing her lips as she stiffened, that left only the very real possibility that the lone key hidden in the inside pocket of his jacket was a key to something personal – *somewhere* personal, she huffed quietly. Somewhere like a room at the Long Spur; a private room. Sadie Shaw's room? Oh, yes, she thought, with a satisfied glint in her eyes, almost certainly Sadie Shaw's room!

She took a step closer to the window, her gaze turning slowly to the left where the main street tightened under its clutter of buildings, culminating in the sprawl of the Long Spur saloon.

Sadie Shaw's room would be one of the half-dozen or so overlooking the rear. Easy enough to reach if you chose your moment to climb the outside stairway. Soon after dark would be a good time, when you might pass through the shadows like a whisper. . . .

Amelia smiled softly to herself as she slipped a hand to the pocket of her dress and let her fingers fondle the cut and shape of the key buried in its depths.

Lucky for her she had found it when she had.

'Some shootin',' murmured Doc Peppers, peering closer at the body of Scully Dyke. 'Fella didn't waste any lead, did he?'

'Just wish he'd waited another ten minutes,' grunted Sam Berrins. 'I was as close to hearin' about

Shard....' He shrugged. 'Too damned late. But you reckon he was here last night?'

'Somebody broke into Henry Clarke's shack out back. And if that somebody was Shard, well, he'd have been around to hear of the shootin' at the saloon, and the arrest of Dyke. And if Dyke was teamin' up with Shard on some planned hit someplace.... Well, we're gettin' a sniff of the answers, aren't we?'

Sam scratched the dirt from his neck. 'A sniff's about it!' he said wearily.

'Yuh heard of this fella Shard?' asked Doc.

'Not in my territory.'

'That'd figure. Scumbag earned his reputation way out East. Rode as a kid with the Downer clan, then along of Frank Smithson and Clay Ward. Murder, rape, robbery, they all came the same to Shard.'

Doc removed his spectacles, folded them and tapped them thoughtfully on the point of his chin. 'Got careless out Sandy Rocks way; shot up a homestead and got caught doin' it. That's how he came to be in the Pen at Kee Mounts.' He glanced quickly at the sheriff. 'But there's somethin' don't make sense here.'

'Whole heap don't make sense!' scoffed Sam.

'Why would a sonofabitch gunslinger as hard-hittin' as Lucas Shard bother with a place like Bedrock?' Doc raised his eyebrows quizzically. 'Playin' plains' wolf? Sneakin' into shacks for a handful of beans? Pinnin' notes to store counters? This the same fella Clay Ward once described as squirmin'' in dirt not even a rattler's slid through? Yuh reckon?'

'No sayin' to it, Doc,' said Sam, leading the trail mount carrying the body of Dyke in the direction of the undertakers. 'But I sure as hell have a gut feelin' we're fast soon goin' to find out. Meantime, I got a body here to bury.'

'Sure,' muttered Doc, stepping back to his porch. 'Best get used to it!'

What few hours were left of that day passed peacefully enough in windswept Bedrock.

Henry Clarke never left his store, not even for his customary lunch at the Long Spur. Lawson Ridges pondered once again on how his future might shape up given the fortuitous windfall of new riches, but came to no positive conclusions, save the promise to himself to keep an extremely close eye on Mayor Carfax. The man was developing worrying bouts of nerves. Sadie Shaw would have to work harder on him.

Carfax himself slept soundly until close on noon, and then spent the rest of the daylight hours busying himself with bank business.

His wife, on the other hand, stayed quietly and seemingly dutifully at home. She needed, she had decided, to conserve her energy for her planned after-dark activities and to spend her time mentally rehearsing the detail.

Town talk among the men continued to centre on the shooting of Deputy Baker and, following Sheriff Berrins's surprise return, the killing of Scully Dyke. Was it a fact, some wanted to know, that a whole mangy herd of gunslingers was about to ride through Bedrock; worse, was it posible they might stop?

Sam Berrins was making no comment, save to urge a mark of respect for Frank Baker and to thank those who had helped lay him to rest on Boot Hill. No such regard would be shown at the burying of Scully Dyke.

Doc Peppers fretted over old newspapers and cuttings from times way back. He was not one bit surprised at the regularity of the appearance of the name Shard in reports and accounts of events of a criminal nature.

But the truly short straw of that day fell to Billy Twine, the long-standing butt of town jokes and banter as a result of his drinking exploits at the Long Spur.

It was as he staggered from the bar, through the batwings and into the street after a particularly indulgent day, that he stood no chance against the pounding hoofs of the mounts of the riders who thundered into town ahead of almost the last wink of sunlight.

Billy was crushed near to death in the riders' reckless rush for the bar, but might have lived had it not been for the leaner, meaner of the three shooting him where he lay in the wind-swirled dirt.

'Do the same for a dog in the circumstances,' he had drawled as he hitched his mount.

And that, as Doc Peppers was to remark later, had been the start of the longest night in Bedrock's history.

SIX

Bedrock erupted into chaos. The street filled with angry men wondering just what sort of a hell it was had ridden in from the wind-chafed plains; with distraught and bewildered women unable to believe, even in their colourful experiences, the manner of the death of Billy Twine, and for no good reason save that he had left the Long Spur when he had.

'Shot him like a dog, they did,' the cry went up, followed by, 'Who the hell are the sonsofbitches anyway?'

Lawson Ridges was among the first to have the answer as the trio stomped, dust and dirt covered, into the bar, the trail filth and smells lifting from them like the stench from a suddenly disturbed heap of trash, then swaggered to the bar with their demands for whiskey and beer pouring from their mouths in a flood of curses.

'You fellas hold up there some,' Ridges had begun, emerging from his private rooms in a flurry of jacket and cigar smoke.

But that had been the sum total of his protest as, once again, the leaner, meaner-looking of the three stepped to Ridges' side and brought the barrel of a Colt clean across the proprietor's temple.

'Catch up on yuh sleep, mister!' the man had drawled, watching Ridges slump to the floor.

'Goddammit, Nate, if you ain't just one helluva busy fella round here, and yuh ain't been in town five minutes,' tittered the younger gunslinger.

Nate merely grinned and thudded a fist to the bar.

'And Crissake don't bring me no gut-twistin' sourmash,' said the elder of the trio, circling the bar like a curious dog. 'Where's the women?'

The hovering pot-man explained as how Miss Sadie and the girls were not usually expected to put in an appearance until after eight.

The elder man had spat defiantly across the room to a spittoon and ordered the pot-man to 'go tell Miss Sadie as how Duke Mabbutt is in town, along of his very good friends, Nate Connors and the Idaho Kid, and that we ain't used to bein' kept waitin', and ain't got the time anyhow. You do that, fella?'

'Sure, I can,' blinked the pot-man.

'Well, you get along and do it, right now, before I change my mind and blast them jack-rabbit ears of yours clean off yuh head!'

It was a full three minutes before Doc Peppers arrived at the body of Billy Twine and pronounced him dead, shot through the head at close range.

Sheriff Sam Berrins stood in the shadow as Doc came wearily upright, the single, sighing phrase 'What in the name of Hell . . .' drifting from his lips as if in echo of the watching faces around him.

'They're in the bar, Sheriff,' said a man in the crowd. 'Three of 'em. Thin fella did the shootin' here.'

'I'll stand to you,' murmured Henry Clarke at Sam's side.

'Me, too,' added Casey Pike.

'What's scum the likes of them doin' in town, anyhow?' asked another man. 'What we want with 'em?'

'What they want with us, f'Crissake – beggin' yuh pardon, ladies?'

'All right, let's just keep this calm, shall we?' said Sam.

'Keep it calm, you say,' protested a woman. 'That's askin' some, Sam Berrins, and no mistake. Could never say a deal in Billy Twine's favour, but come the reckonin', he was human and didn't deserve to die like that.' The crowd voiced its support. 'And just where is the mayor in all of this?' clipped the woman indignantly.

'He's right here,' said Newton Carfax from the shadowed boardwalk. 'Yuh got my full backin' for whatever yuh got to do, Sam.'

'Well, ain't that mighty big of him!' muttered Doc Peppers.

'So what we waitin' for?' grunted an oldster.

'Let's go settle it,' urged a youth.

'Steady up there,' ordered Sam, stepping aside, his back to the bar and batwings.

'Some of yuh are sure as hell keen to get among the lead,' said Casey Pike. 'T'ain't that easy to step up there. Yuh can't just go—'

'Cut the sermonizin', Casey,' came the call. 'Why don't we get to a hangin'? Straight out murder we got here, ain't it?'

'There'll be no lynchin' in my town,' snapped the mayor. 'We leave this matter to the law - and Sam Berrins is our duly elected and appointed sheriff. So I say we. . . .'

Carfax's voice trailed away to an inaudible grunt and moan as the batwings creaked open and a heavy, demanding boot hit the boardwalk.

'Lucas Shard in town yet?' growled the elderly gunslinger, twirling a Colt through his grubby fingers.

'Duke Mabbutt,' murmured Sam Berrins to himself as he turned and stared into the face of the man.

'You know this scumbag, Sam?' whispered Doc. 'I got newspaper cuttin's on him. Rides with a coupla others.'

'Nate Connors and the Idaho Kid.'

'That's them. Operate south of here. So where's the tie-in with Shard?'

'We're about to find out,' said Sam, taking a step to the boardwalk.

'Well, now,' grinned Mabbutt, steadying the Colt, 'look who we got here – Sheriff Sam Berrins, as ever was. How yuh doin', Sam?'

'No better for clappin' eyes on you, Duke.'

'That ain't no way to greet an old friend.'

'No friend, Duke. Not now, not ever.' Sam's gaze tightened. 'You responsible for this?' he added, nodding to the body of Billy Twine.

'Me?' gestured Mabbutt, his grin spreading. 'Would I do that? You know me for better, Sam Berrins. No, t'ain't my doin'. That's Nate's work. He don't change none. Shoots first, thinks it through later.'

'That's murder, anywhich way yuh see it. Goin' to have to take him in, Duke. Don't have no choice.'

Sam took another step to the boardwalk, only to freeze on the steely click of Mabbutt's Colt.

'Whoa there, Sam,' grunted Mabbutt. 'Yuh ain't takin' nobody in, so let's just get that clear. We go back some time, mister. Texas days, eh? Don't let's get to spoilin' a beautiful friendship.' He ranged the Colt menacingly. 'I ain't for shootin' yuh, Sam. Stand back there if yuh got any sense.'

Sam stiffened, but stood his ground, Doc Peppers fuming quietly at his shoulder. He was conscious of Henry Clarke and Casey Pike easing to his back, of the tensed, stretched silence among the townfolk.

'Fella Nate shot didn't look to be much, anyhow,' sneered Mabbutt, the Colt still levelled. 'Too much coffin varnish in him by the look of it. So what's it matter, eh? Don't count for a snitch. More to the point—'

'What yuh doin' here, Duke?' said Sam. 'What yuh want? And what's this about Shard?'

'You know Lucas Shard?' asked Mabbutt.

'Heard some, but he ain't here. Never has been.'

Mabbutt's eyes narrowed darkly. 'You sure about that?' he growled. 'You wouldn't be lyin' to me now, would you, Sam?'

'We had a fella prowlin' round town for three

whole days,' called somebody in the crowd.

'Hell!' hissed Doc, craning to identify the voice.

'And what about the note and the break-in at the store?' shouted another.

The street gathering murmured, Doc cringed and ran a hand over his face. 'Of all the stupid . . .' he moaned quietly.

'Of no account,' said Sam lightly and without a deal of conviction.

'Fella wrote his name on the note, didn't he?' persisted the voice. 'Weren't that Shard? Tell him, Henry. Go on, tell him, f'Crissake.'

The crowd's murmurings deepened. Doc sighed. Sam Berrins bit at his lip. Casey Pike clenched his fists.

'So,' grinned Mabbutt, twirling the Colt again, 'seems like yuh ain't been quite straight with me here, Sam.' He tut-tutted. 'That ain't no way to show yuh friendship, is it? Why, for two pins I'd—'

'I am the town mayor here,' announced Carfax, shouldering his way to the sheriff's side, 'and I want to make it perfectly clear that if you would like to state your business and make your requirements known to us, I am sure that, within reason, we shall be more than happy to co-operate. Not, you understand, that we are in any way condonin' what's happened here this evenin' or excusin' it. But, like I say—'

'Speak for y'self, Newton!' hissed Doc in the mayor's ear.

'Yuh got some mouth on yuh there, Mr Mayor,' sneered Mabbutt. 'Well, what yuh say, Sam, yuh goin' to co-operate like the mayor says, or ain't yuh?'

'Don't do it, Sam,' hissed Doc again.

Sam pulled at his collar in the swirl of the wind. A lantern flickered to send the street shadows scurrying. A man coughed. Somebody sniffed. 'Well?' asked the indignant woman, folding her arms. Sam pulled the other side of his collar.

'Prowlin' fella was just a drifter,' said Doc hurriedly, breaking the silence as if stepping on it. 'Scavengin' type; plains' wolf, yuh might say. We get any number of 'em this time of the year. Drift across the Seroquoi like so much trash on the wind. He weren't nobody. I seen him.'

'Same here,' enthused Henry. 'I seen him. Sure I did. Broke into my store for somethin' to eat. Helped himself to beans. That's all. Nothin' of consequence. Like the doc says, they blow in on the wind. Shan't see that fella again.'

'What about the note?' persisted the voice.

'Note?' shrugged Henry. 'I didn't see no note. You see a note, Doc?'

'Not a scrap,' said Doc.

'Gentlemen, this is gettin' us nowhere,' began Carfax again. 'Why don't we step inside the saloon and get to discussin' this sensibly and logically over a bottle—'

'And what about that gunslinger got shot this mornin', Sheriff?' the voice ranted on, drowning out the mayor as the others grunted their encouragement. 'Scully Dyke, weren't it? What about him? He tied in with all this?'

Mabbutt twirled the Colt and stared icily into

Sam's face. 'This is gettin' deeper and deeper, ain't it? So what's this with Dyke? You ain't tellin' me, are yuh, as how yuh been tanglin' with my good friend Scully?'

The batwings creaked open to the shape of the youngest of the gunslingers.

'What yuh want, Kid?' growled Mabbutt.

'We got ourselves some gals here, Duke,' smiled the youngster, 'and they sure as hell need some tamin', so why don't yuh—'

The shot broke through the gloom and the sounds of the sneaking, snivelling wind like something spat from the night sky. The Idaho Kid's hands spread across his chest, the blood already bubbling between the fingers, his eyes suddenly wide and rolling in the few seconds he swayed where he stood on the boardwalk before pitching headlong into the dirt-swirled street.

The crowd gasped. Duke Mabbutt stared in disbelief. And the plains' wind moaned through every nook and cranny it could find.

SEVEN

Sam Berrins had cleared the street within minutes. Doc Peppers had pronounced the Idaho Kid dead without so much as troubling to bend close to the body. The mayor had sweated, gazed round him as if struck dumb by some sudden fever and dived through the batwings in search of the nearest bottle, and Duke Mabbutt had emptied the chamber of his brandished Colt in a frenzy of wild shooting.

The shots and the general mayhem had brought Nate Connors to the boardwalk where he simply stood, his gaze tight and narrowed, scanning every inch of every shape, window, doorway he could make out against the glow of night lanterns on the darkness.

A group of the bar girls had panicked and tumbled through the 'wings like a fluttering of moths. Lawson Ridges had stirred to a dazed consciousness and thought he was still deep in some nightmare.

And Amelia Carfax, seizing her opportunity while the town busied itself with the new arrivals, had passed unseen and unheard through the dark alley to the stairs to the first-floor rooms at the Long Spur, reached the deserted corridor and the door to Sadie Shaw's quarters, and inserted the key she had taken from her husband's pocket in the lock – only to find it did not fit.

Now, with the bar below her beginning to fill and the girls herded towards the stairs, she had no hope of returning to the back alley by the way she had come. In fact, she was beginning to realize in the chill of a cold sweat trickling down her spine, she had nowhere to go and could only wait where she shuddered.

'Inside, Sheriff,' growled Mabbutt, gesturing with his reloaded Colt for Sam to step through the 'wings to the bar. 'We got some serious talkin' to do, and I sure as hell hope for your sake yuh got some explanation for all this!' He swung round to face Doc and Henry Clarke. 'You get that body to the undertakers, and you tell the fella there I want the best there is for the Kid. Yuh understand? No cheap pine; proper handles and that. Get to it!'

'Well,' said Henry, when the body had been delivered and he and Doc were alone again in the now deserted street, 'what yuh reckon? Who fired that shot? Couldn't have been Shard. He wouldn't go killin' his own kind. So just who is it we got prowlin' round town? And was he out there on the plain to shoot Scully Dyke? And what's with them scum at the saloon, what we goin' to do about them?'

'Hold on, Henry,' sighed Doc, running a finger round the inside of his collar, 'first things first. We should look to Sam. Can't leave him to stand alone there.' He adjusted his hat. 'As for who did the shootin' – I agree, hardly likely to have been Shard, which leaves us. . . .' He shrugged. 'Leaves us precisely nowhere. I just wouldn't have a clue, but that ain't to say we stop watchin' for him, whoever, wherever he is. He might be gettin' hungry again, so yuh'd best get back to your store in case he shows there. I'll join Sam.'

'Whole town's gone mad,' groaned Henry. 'I just don't figure what's goin' on.'

'But somebody does,' said Doc, peering down the shadowy street as Casey Pike approached from the livery.

'I've had a visitor!' he hissed, once within earshot. 'Fella's left his horse with me, would yuh believe?'

'The wolf?' frowned Henry.

'Gotta be. I ain't never seen the mount before. T'ain't from these parts, so it's gotta be his. Decent condition too, savin' that it's hungry.'

'That means the fella's stayin',' reflected Doc, rubbing his chin. 'But why? He's gotta be waitin' for Shard.'

'But why the note?' asked Henry.

'A warnin' for us to watch for the scumbag.'

'Hell, must be somethin' big brewin',' grunted Casey. 'But here, in Bedrock? Takes some swallowin' to reckon for that.'

'Them gunslingers back there don't take no swallowin',' said Henry. 'They're real enough. But, damnit, how many guns does Shard want?'

'Well, he'd mebbe best start countin' again,' grinned Doc. 'He's already lost two, and I wouldn't be one bit surprised if our plains' wolf ain't watchin' out right now for his next target.'

The three men fell to silence as their gazes moved slowly over the night-hugged street where only the wind kept them company.

Amelia Carfax had retreated like a petrified insect into the deepest of the shadows in the half-lit corridor. If she could have eaten her way into the woodwork she would have done so gladly. As it was, she could only wait, stiff and straight between tremors, and pray that an opportunity to slip away to the back stairs would come before she finally passed out.

She had taken a ridiculous chance – she knew that now – and to no avail. But if the secret key did not fit the door to Sadie Shaw's room, then whose door did it fit? Some door in another building, in another town perhaps? Or was it, after all, something to do with the bank?

She had been a fool to come to such a hasty conclusion. It might have been better to wait and watch for her husband's reaction when he had realized the key was missing. And that was a possibility that might come sooner than expected, she thought, if for some reason he felt in his jacket for the key while he was there in the bar.

She shivered again. Perhaps it would be better to give herself up right now; walk down the stairs to the saloon with as much regal decorum and nonchalant disregard of the company as she could summon. The look on her husband's face would be almost worth the effort!

The reaction of the unsavoury-looking gunslingers might be another matter.

She listened carefully, straining to catch the lift and fall of the voices. One of the gunslingers, the man they called Duke, was talking – growling more like – at Sheriff Berrins. . . .

'Yuh been a whole sight too busy for my likin'. I ain't much for it. Takin' out Scully like yuh did was a mistake. Yuh shouldn't have done that. Still, we'll leave Shard to sort it out.' Mabbutt spun the Colt through his fingers, then lounged his weight on the bar. 'Meantime, this prowlin' fella they keep on about; what yuh goin' to tell me about him?'

'Go to hell, Mabbutt,' said Sam, the sweat across his brow glistening in the dull lantern light. 'Yuh ain't welcome here, and now you've lost the Kid I suggest yuh move on fast.'

'Do yuh now?' sneered the gunslinger. He turned to his partner. 'Yuh hear that, Nate? Sheriff here's gettin' lippy.'

Connors gulped a measure of whiskey and thudded the glass to the bar. 'Somebody pays in my book for the Kid dyin' like that.'

'You're right,' grinned Mabbutt, 'somebody does. So who's it goin' to be, Sam? Who we got stalkin' around with a lethal Winchester crooked in his arm?

Yuh goin' to bring him outa the woodwork, or are me and Nate here goin' to have to persuade yuh?'

'We should get to lookin' at this matter afresh,' began Carfax importantly, brushing a hand over his brocade waistcoat. 'We are probably as much in the dark about this prowlin' drifter as you are, Mr Mabbutt. We have certainly never got to speakin' with him, and as for the shootin'—'

Mabbutt kicked a chair into the mayor's shins. 'Yuh talk too much,' he growled, levelling the Colt.

'Now wait,' groaned Lawson Ridges from the shadows. 'Just hold it before there's more blood spilled.' He blinked dazedly. 'Let's just tell 'em what we know, Sam, and leave it at that. Hell, I ain't never known so much activity in Bedrock. So what's so special about us all of a sudden? What we done to deserve this attention?' His gaze swung from Sam, to the few drinkers still marooned in the bar, to Mabbutt and Connors, then back to settle on Mabbutt's expressionless face. 'Well,' he croaked, 'what yuh want with us, mister?'

Sam's stare narrowed and tightened. Carfax shifted uncomfortably. The bar girls gazed wide-eyed and silent. Doc Peppers slid through the batwings and into the bar with barely a creak of hinge or board. Nate Connors poured himself another measure from the whiskey bottle.

'None of yuh business,' said Mabbutt, the Colt flat and still in his grip. 'Yuh just do as you're told for as long as I say, 'til Shard gets here. But right now' – he levelled the gun at Sam – 'yuh unbuckle that belt, Sheriff, and Nate here'll see if he can bed yuh down real comfortable in one of your own cells. Keep yuh out of mischief, eh?'

He grinned and pushed himself clear of the bar. 'Rest of yuh relax. Nobody goes no place 'ceptin' on my say so. Yuh got that? Yuh just think things through, 'cus I'm tellin' yuh straight up that if we ain't a whole lot closer to nailin' the rat who did for the Kid out there come first light, I'm goin' to start extractin' a helluva payment in recompense. I'll shoot somebody every hour, on the hour. Got it? So like I say, relax and think it through.'

Sam Berrins stiffened and sweated. Carfax shivered and tugged at his waistcoat. Lawson Ridges blinked and winced at the throb in his head. The bar girls turned pale. Doc Peppers eased himself into a chair at an empty table facing the stairs and was the only one who saw Amelia Carfax pass like a shadow along the corridor above the bar.

Just what in tarnation was she doing here in the saloon, he wondered, and why, in Heaven's name, in the area of the girls' quarters? No place for the mayor's wife. No place for the mayor, come to that. But for Mrs Carfax to be there at a time like this when just about—

The Winchester spat and blazed again, somewhere in the street, shattering the lantern above the batwings and plunging the boardwalk into darkness.

'Hell!' mouthed Doc, his thoughts of Amelia Carfax dismissed in the drift and smell of fresh gunsmoke.

EIGHT

'He's still here,' hissed Newton Carfax, sidling into a shadowed corner of the bar where Lawson Ridges was already trying to hide. 'The prowler, plains' wolf – call him what yuh will – he ain't left. Who is he? What's he want?'

'How the hell should I know?' grunted Ridges, his gaze dancing round the bar, to Mabbutt and Connors, to the batwings and the darkened boardwalk beyond.

'Sam Berrins just goin' to stand there? What's Doc plannin'? Them gunslingers movin' again? I just wish somebody would get to tellin' me what in the name of sanity is goin' on.'

'That's just it, yuh fool, there ain't no sanity!' snapped Ridges. 'Not since Scully Dyke rode in; not since this fella Mabbutt and his sidekicks showed up. I tell yuh, Newton, it's time we made a move.'

'What yuh sayin?' hissed Carfax again, the sweat beginning to bead across his brow.

Plains' Wolf

'I'm sayin' it's time we took the money yuh got stashed and pulled out. Clear town fast. I'm plannin' on headin' south. Best do it now before this whole situation gets any worse. And especially before any more of the likes of Mabbutt get to imposin' themselves.'

Carfax blinked rapidly on the thin lantern-light, his eyes like moons in the shadows. 'Can't do that at the drop of a hat,' he croaked. 'Can't just take the money, saddle up, ride out.'

'Why? You tell me why we can't do just that. Yuh got the money, ain't yuh? It's there, in the bank. *Your bank*. What's to stop us takin' it now? Tonight. Been sittin' on it long enough.'

'Put like that, o'course . . .' shrugged Carfax. 'But there's this place. . . . There's my wife.'

'This place ain't no better, no worse, than a dozen others I could name. I could open a Long Spur any place, anytime, and one helluva sight more profitable with the money comin' my way. As for your wife, since when yuh been concernin' yourself with her well-bein'?'

Ridges laid a hand on the mayor's arm as Mabbutt and Connors took up position either side of the batwings.

'They steppin' out to the street?' whispered Carfax. 'Mebbe they're goin' in search of the prowler.'

'Not in the dark, they ain't. They ain't that stupid. No, they'll wait 'til first light – and that, my friend, is when we make our move.'

Carfax swallowed. 'Well . . .' he began, licking at sweat.

'No ponderin' on it, Newton. We do it. We're out of town at dawn. Now, where yuh holdin' the money exactly? It difficult to get at?'

'Not for me, it ain't. Brought in a special safe, fixed tight to the floor in my office. Ain't nobody could shift that safe, not no how. Yuh'd have to blast it where it stands, and even then—'

'Sure, sure, I get the message,' tempered Ridges. 'Point is, have yuh got the key and can the money be moved?'

Carfax stiffened. ' 'Course I got the key. Carry it personally. Right here in my pocket.' He made to delve for it, but hesitated at Ridges' grip on his arm.

'Don't go showin' it around, yuh fool! Somebody might be watchin'. Doc Peppers there, for instance.'

Carfax glanced anxiously round the saloon. 'Right,' he murmured. 'Point made and taken. As for movin' the money, it's goin' to take time and we're goin' to need a pack horse.'

'That much to carry, eh?' smiled Ridges. 'Well, now. . . . Leave the horse to me. You get to the money soon as you can. Transfer it to bags tonight, and join me here again when you're all through.'

'And just how the hell am I supposed to get out of here without them scumbags fillin' me full of lead? Yuh figured that?'

'Not yet,' said Ridges, his eyes narrowing to slits, 'but I'm workin' on it. I'm workin' on it. . . .'

Doc Peppers filled his pipe carefully, slowly, taking care to tamp the baccy to an even level as his gaze above the spectacles perched on his nose roved round the bar.

Nothing Sam Berrins could do but wait, he thought, watching the sheriff fume quietly. Same went for Ridges and Carfax, though they seemed to be finding plenty to discuss back there in the shadows. He just hoped they were not hatching another of Carfax's town plans. Most of them only ever came to grief.

Which reminded him – what had happened to the mayor's wife?

His gaze shifted to the stairs, the bar girls huddled at the foot of them, and then moved higher to the shadow-filled but now deserted corridor. No sign of Mrs Carfax. So, had she left by the back stairs, smuggled herself out of sight in one of the rooms – unlikely, he thought, they were always kept locked – or was she still up there, too scared to move?

Damn it, what had she been doing there in the first place?

Doc's gaze moved away, across the bar to the batwings and the tensed, waiting shapes of Duke Mabbutt and Nate Connors.

Stand there watching the boardwalk and the empty street for as long as they had the patience for, he reflected, but they would be wasting their time. Fellow with the Winchester would not be for showing himself, not this side of sun-up. Probably sleeping some place safe. He had done enough for one night. Mabbutt and his sidekick could do all the waiting and watching!

Doc lit his pipe, leaned back from the curling

cloud of smoke and winked reassuringly at one of the pale-faced bar girls.

Going to be a long night for all concerned, he reckoned.

'Yuh said for this bein' easy money,' grumbled Connors, his mean gaze slanted on his partner on the other side of the batwings. 'I ain't seein' it that way – and we lost the Kid into the bargain. Some deal eh? Yuh still figurin' it for bein' easy?' He ran his tongue noisily over his cracked, dirt-smeared lips. 'We should've kept ridin', yuh know that? And what's with this Shard? Why ain't he shown?'

'You all through moanin' there, mister?' said Mabbutt, his own gaze still ranging the dark, empty street beyond the boardwalk. 'You're a whole sight worse than a wailin' whore. So we lost the Kid – he had it comin' for months. Gettin' too smart. Too much mouth. If it hadn't been here, it'd have been the next town.' He spat over the 'wings to the boards. 'Kid ain't no loss – and we get to splittin' his share, don't we? Yuh thought of that in all yuh moanin'?'

'Won't be no money 'til Shard turns up, will there?'

'This is Shard's show. He'll be here.'

Connors grunted and scanned the street. 'And what about the sonofabitch out there givin' us all this trouble? What we goin' to do about him?'

'What are *you* goin' to do about him!' grinned Mabbutt. 'Strikes me you're in need of some action, Nate, so why don't yuh go take a walk about town, see what yuh can see?'

'What about the sheriff there?'

'We'll lock him up later. He ain't no trouble for now. You just get out there, eh? Go earn some of that easy money.'

Connors holstered his Colt and tipped the brim of his hat. 'I set an eye on that Winchester rat, I'll skin him. Then shoot him!'

'That's my boy!' smiled Mabbutt.

Amelia Carfax pushed the strands of her wind-tousled hair from her face and backed deep into the shadows of the doorway. She was not sure she could go on. She should never have started. She should be at home; anywhere but here in the street, lurking in the night like some cheap town tart. She was ashamed – and she just hoped nobody had seen her leave the Long Spur by the back stairs. The tongues would never stop wagging, and the looks . . . oh, the looks would kill at twenty yards!

She was also shivering, sweating, bewildered and scared.

She could not understand what was happening to the town. Bedrock had always been such a quiet place; nothing much ever happened; nothing much ever *wanted* to happen. And the folk were easy-going, sometimes a touch boring and lacking the spirit of adventure, but honest if nothing else.

And she could not understand either what was happening to her husband. Oh, she knew about his dalliances and indulgences – she would soon have him paying a price for those – but she could not fathom that suddenly distant, preoccupied look in his eyes, the deepening association with Lawson Ridges (which went far beyond his provision of women, Sadie Shaw in particular, she suspected) and nor could she explain the key.

It had not fitted the lock on the door to Sadie's room. That did not make sense, because if she had been mistaken in her assumption at the outset and the key was, in fact, a part of the bunch that served the bank, then why had it been separated and hidden in the deepest reaches of the jacket pocket?

She could, of course, return the key to the pocket at the next opportunity and leave the matter there. She could confront her husband with it and insist on an explanation. But that would expose her as a wife who nosied into her husband's pockets. Or she could keep the key; see how long it would be before Newton noticed it was missing.

She smiled softly to herself in spite of her discomfort. The notion of her husband squirming for a few days rather appealed to her. It might teach him a lesson; might make him realize. . . .

She gasped on a sudden intake of breath at the banging of a door in the bristling wind. Time she was gone, she thought, pushing her hair from her face again. Time she was home, warm and comfortable, beyond the reach of whatever madness it was had gripped the town.

She arranged the shawl across her shoulders, tied it, smoothed the folds of her long, pleated dress and stepped from the doorway.

But it was only a half step, one she never completed before the hands had clawed from the darkness, covering her mouth, dragging her back beyond the doorway and into the cluttered alley at the rear of the long abandoned gunsmiths.

'Now just what have I got m'self here?' growled the voice across the squalling wind as the man's grip tightened and Amelia Carfax's head began to spin.

NINE

Casey Pike eased to the deepest of the shadows cast by the lantern glow in his living area at the livery, listened for a moment, caught nothing above the familiar gentle snort of a stabled horse, the scuff of a hoof through straw, and relaxed again.

He had been mistaken, there had been no creak that might have been a careful footfall. There was nothing out there in the stabling save horses. The man – the prowler, the plains' wolf – had not returned to collect his horse. Wherever he was holed up in town, he was staying put, certainly for tonight. Tomorrow was another day and a whole new prospect, especially here in Bedrock where things, and folk too in some cases, had a habit of shifting by the hour.

And as if Scully Dyke had not been bad news and smell enough, they now had the likes of Duke Mabbutt and Nate Connors fouling the street, with little hope, it seemed, of the situation changing until Shard arrived. And when that happened.... Well, now, who could say?

He swallowed, blinked, shifted his position, and listened again. Definitely mistaken, he decided, and eased back to the table in the full glow of the lantern-light.

Time to go check on Henry at the store; take a look – from a safe distance – at the saloon, see if Doc needed a hand, and then, if he was still of the same mind, maybe make his own tour of the town. Sam Berrins was probably going to be under close watch for as long as it suited Mabbutt, but there was nothing to stop the town blacksmith from going about his business, was there?

Mabbutt could not be watching everybody all of the time; same went for Connors. So the quiet hours of darkness might be just the time to go probing for mysterious 'visitors' who took to stabling their mounts without warning.

Somebody had to try to make contact with the man with the Winchester, if only to urge him not to ride out!

Twenty minutes later, Casey had checked in with Henry – 'All quiet here,' he had reported – and taken his good advice to steer clear of the Long Spur.

'Winchester fella's blasted the boardwalk light and set them rats into bein' real watchful,' Henry had warned. 'I reckon Connors is roamin' around. Wouldn't want yuh to cross him. Best get y'self back to your place. We ain't goin' to solve nothin' of this 'til Shard gets here, and that might be anytime. Meanwhile, they're holdin' Sam; Doc's just keepin' watch; Ridges ain't doin' nothin'; and that so-called mayor of ours is doin' even less! Tell yuh somethin' now, Casey, we get through this in one piece and there's goin' to be some real shake-ups hereabouts. You can bet on it.'

Well, maybe there would at that, agreed Casey, but that was speculation, not the now, tonight, with somebody on the loose out there in the wind-strafed street with a sharp aim and a still sharper finger on the trigger of his rifle.

But just where, he wondered, buttoning his coat to his neck as he left the store and stepped to the boardwalk?

He stared into the pitch-black night to left and right, peering tighter where the few lights still burning cast their glow and spread the shadows. He would hardly reckon for the fellow staying close to the street, and certainly not within gun range of the saloon. No, he would be lurking some place back of the main street, among the clutter of outbuildings, shacks and lean-tos, where men stacked their flotsam and figured for it being left for dust.

Guilty as the rest, he thought, slipping away to the rear of the store, cursing through clenched teeth as he cracked a shin on a length of planking, paused mid step for a moment to catch his breath – and heard the muffled noise.

It might have been a voice, but there had been no call, no words; might have been a gasp, another nosy citizen cracking his shin, but there had been just a hint of desperation in the sound, as if somebody – and not too far away at that, reckoned Casey – had been trying to shout.

Somebody who had been quickly silenced.

Casey waited until there was only the howl and crack of the wind before moving on, this time turning left, through the ever-deepening clutter towards the abandoned gunsmith's store. Once been the business of Zac Potter, he recalled; ten or more years till Zac took ill and had died alone. No kin to carry the business on, and so it had finally closed its doors for the last time and the place been left to the wind and dirt.

Shame, he thought, decent building like that just abandoned. . . .

There it was again, the muffled noise; scuffing along of it now, reckoned Casey, pausing instantly as he pressed himself tight to the wall of a leaning shack. Not far away now. Must be in Zac's old place.

Was that where the plains' prowler was holed up? If so, he had company, and not overly welcome at that by the sound of it.

Casey moved on, one soft step at a time, inching his way through the darkness like an anxious spider, annoyed now that he had not had the good sense to strap on a gunbelt, collect his rifle, arm himself in some way, however slight.

So maybe he should go back to the store, get Henry's help, at least borrow a gun from him. But, what the hell, fellow would have slipped away by then. If it was the prowler up there, he was not at this moment aware of Casey's approach.

Could be he was ripe for being taken by surprise for once.

*

It was the eyes he saw first: round, very bright and mirroring the fear of a very scared woman, thought Casey, swallowing, blinking, reaching for both hand and footholds as he fumbled and stumbled through the open doorway of the gunsmith's.

'Mrs Carfax?' he croaked ridiculously, knowing full well that the gag tied across her mouth would prevent an answer, and staring in disbelief at her roped, dishevelled body slumped in the corner of the empty room. 'What the hell in tarnation is goin' on?' he began again, stumbling forward, blinking on the darkness, the faint, shafted light.

The woman groaned, squirmed, stared as Casey approached, her eyes flashing on the words she could not form, the grunts that made no sense.

'Wouldn't want to be around when the mayor gets to hear—'

Casey's voice died in his throat. His head filled and reeled in a swirl of flashes. Thoughts were drowned instantly and only the pain burned for the moments it took for him to slide to the floor in a crumpled heap.

Nate Connors eased from the shadows, spun his Colt, holstered it and grinned at Amelia Carfax.

'Guess this nosyin' intruder here is set to sleep some, yuh reckon?' he drawled, his gaze gleaming, the grin spreading, as he lifted his eyes from the body to the woman. 'Long enough for us to give this another try, eh? Get that gag from yuh pretty mouth so's you can start tellin' me all about this.'

He dangled the key taken from Newton Carfax's jacket between his fingers. 'Sure set some store by it, don't yuh, ma'am? Well, that bein' so, I'm all for yuh sharin' it. Agreed? Yuh goin' to do that?'

Amelia Carfax's eyes could not have grown rounder.

TEN

'Soon as I make a move for the back room, yuh follow. Got it? Just keep right in my tracks,' whispered Ridges into Newton Carfax's sweating face. 'Minute we're into my office, you disappear through the door to the alley and get to doin' what's necessary, fast as yuh can. Any luck and we could be gone before noon.'

'I just hope this is goin' to work,' murmured Carfax, wiping his face. 'It's one helluva risk.'

' 'Course it'll work. We don't get to that money t'night and start loadin' it we might never get to it. Shard will see to that. He won't be the sort to turn up his nose at a safe full of money, no matter what he's come to Bedrock for. We can't give him or anybody else so much as half a chance. So yuh pull y'self t'gether and follow me. Right?'

Carfax sighed, stiffened and nodded, then turned from the bar to gaze quickly over the saloon. Mabbutt was still watching the street from the batwings. No sign as yet of Connors returning. Doc was still at his table, his concentration settled, it seemed, on the performance of his pipe. Sam Berrins simply fumed and sweated. The bar girls stayed huddled, Sadie Shaw hovering over them like a mother hen. The few drinkers remained sober, simply watching, wondering, waiting. The bar clock's tick hung on dull echoes, and even the smoke haze lingered as if uncertain of where to go.

Ridges cleared his throat importantly. 'Need to get to my office there,' he announced, beginning to move.

'Hold it right where yuh are, mister,' drawled Mabbutt from the 'wings, his gaze not shifting from the street. 'Yuh don't go nowhere save when I say yuh do. Simple as that.'

'Damn it, all I want to do is go to my office,' flared Ridges. 'It's my saloon, remember, my office, and I ain't leavin' the buildin' exactly, am I?'

'But yuh might,' sneered Mabbutt. 'Yuh just might – 'cus you're the type that does that sorta thing.' He swung his gaze from the night. 'So yuh just sit tight some place, mister, 'til I decide other.'

'This is an outrage,' spluttered Carfax.

'Be a whole sight more if yuh don't do just as I'm tellin' yuh, Mr Mayor,' said Mabbutt, his attention on the street again. 'I ain't one bit fussed as to who folk are. All get treated the same. And that includes you. Especially you. Sit down!'

'You plannin' on keepin' us here all night?' asked Sam.

'I plan on keepin' yuh here for just as long as it suits, Sheriff.' Mabbutt laid the barrel of his Colt across the top of the batwings. 'Yuh ain't objectin', are yuh?'

'Seems to me—' began Sam.

'I don't give a damn what it may or may not seem to you or anybody else. I got a scumbag sniper out there with an itchy finger to a Winchester, and that I do not like. Not one bit. So, 'til he's taken care of, yuh stay. No arguin'.'

'Or this fella Shard turns up,' said Sam carefully, conscious of Doc's gaze shifting to Mabbutt. 'Just when exactly are yuh expectin' him?'

'None of your business. But seein' as how you're the lawman round here, I'd reckon on yuh welcomin' him come sun-up. That suit?'

'Long time to sun-up.' shrugged Sam. 'He ridin' through the night? Hell, that's a touch dangerous across the Seroquoi. Never easy, even in full light, but in the dark with the big blow just findin' its lungs, well, now, I wouldn't—'

'Never mind the wind out there on the plain, Sheriff,' sneered Mabbutt again, 'you just take a look here what it's blowin' in right now down your own street. Step up here,' he gestured, a grin sliding across his face. 'What yuh see there? Who's the fancy woman Nate's found himself? Yuh know her? Sure yuh do, I'll bet. And from the look on Nate's face, I'd say we're in for an entertainin' few hours, wouldn't you?'

Sam's stomach churned to a chilled emptiness as he stared into the street.

Newton Carfax's face had undergone a deathly change of colour that had drained it of blood until the flesh was stretched across his cheekbones like some worn, yellowed parchment that might disintegrate to dust at any moment. And for once in his life he was speechless. He could only stare at his wife as if seeing a ghost.

Amelia Carfax had passed from nightmare to hell fire and come full circle back to nightmare. She stood in the smoky, liquor-hazed gloom of the Long Spur saloon bar in a dazed, silent, impossible world of her own, unaware now of Connors, of faces and the place, and probably deaf to the sound of the voices around her.

'Give me that again,' growled Mabbutt, his eyes blinking on a surge of sweat as he stared into Nate Connors' face. 'And keep it slow and steady. No rush. I want the details, every last one.'

Connors lifted a whiskey bottle to his lips, gulped on the liquor, groaned, spat, wiped a hand across his mouth and giggled for a moment like a child. 'I tell yuh, Duke, it was that simple, just like I told yuh: found this woman here skulkin' in the street; no idea who she was, o'course, but good-lookin', so I figures I might have m'self some fun for a while; drags her into a shack, and that's when the key yuh got there falls from her dress. But, hell, did she fight some to get her hands on it again. Did she! Which kinda set me to reckonin' that it might, just might, be a very important key, special to somewhere. Get my meanin'?'

Carfax shivered. Lawson Ridges shot him an uneasy glance. Doc Peppers watched the woman, ready to spring to his feet the second her eyes glazed.

Sam Berrins ran his sticky hands down his pants. The bar girls did not move. The drinkers had stopped drinking.

'Go on,' grunted Mabbutt.

'So,' Connors went on, after another gulp from the bottle, 'I gets to persuadin' the lady to tell me all about the key. Didn't do her no harm as yuh can see. Well, nothin' that won't heal. Anyhow, she tells me as how the key belongs to her husband – Mr Mayor there *and* sole owner no less of the bank here in Bedrock. Lady didn't say how she'd come by the key or why, but I can imagine.

'Well, now,' swaggered Connors, raising the bottle again, 'didn't take no genius figurin' to reckon for *that* key bein' somethin' to do with *that* bank across there. And if that's the case. . . . What yuh say, Duke, key to a safe?'

Mabbutt turned the key softly through his fingers, his gaze on it like a light. 'You tell me, Mr Mayor,' he murmured.

'That key has absolutely nothin' to do with you,' blustered Carfax. 'My wife had no right, none at all, to have it on her person. She must have. . . . But that's another matter. The fact is—'

'Fact is, Mr Mayor,' said Mabbutt, coming slowly to his feet from the table, 'you don't get to tellin' me, and showin' me, just what this key is for, that lady of yours is fast goin' to get to lookin' a whole sight worse than she already does. Now, yuh take my advice—'

'Lay a finger on her . . .' snorted Carfax.

'Easy there!' snapped Berrins.

Doc was on his feet as Connors approached the

woman. 'You don't touch her, mister,' he said, 'not unless you're lookin' to hang.'

Connors paused, swigged noisily from the bottle and glared at Amelia Carfax.

'Leave it, Nate,' said Mabbutt. 'Mayor here ain't no fool. He'll do as he's told. Won't yuh?'

Carfax shivered and closed his eyes.

'I hope this ain't leadin' where I think it is,' hissed Ridges in the mayor's ear.

'This whole mess is gettin' way outa hand,' said Sam, beginning to step forward.

But how far the sheriff would have got before either of the gunslingers barred his way would never be known.

Sam ducked instinctively along with the others at the crack and whine of two rifle shots that shattered the mirror at the back of the bar and the lantern on a table to plunge the saloon into darkness.

Tables and chairs were knocked over. The bar girls screamed. Somebody yelled and dived through the 'wings. Connors fired a high, wild shot and Mabbutt cursed.

It was a long three minutes before Lawson Ridges had another lantern lit and the bar was bathed in a flat yellow glow.

But by then Newton Carfax had made good his escape.

ELEVEN

'I'll torch every last stick and plank of the hell-hole! You just watch if I don't. And every last sonofabitch along of it – just for good measure!'

Nate Connors fired three blazing shots high into the night sky and grinned at the whine and pitch of their echoes behind the still blustering plains' wind. 'That'll take care of that yellow-bellied Winchester louse! You bet it will,' he yelled at the top of his voice, as he reloaded his Colt in his straddled stance in the middle of the street.

'Hold it there, yuh darned fool!' shouted Mabbutt from the shadowed boardwalk at the saloon. 'Fella could pick yuh off easy as pluggin' a pail if yuh stand there long enough. Get back here, f'Crissake.'

Connors scowled and slouched reluctantly from the street. 'Where the hell that fancy-tailored mayor go? He don't get himself right back here, I'm goin' to take that wife of his and—'

'No yuh ain't,' growled Mabbutt. 'You're goin' to keep yuh hands off that woman, 'cus we're goin' to need her.'

'Too right we are!'

'As a hostage, yuh dumb-head!'

'How come?' frowned Connors, his voice softer as he stepped closer. 'What yuh plannin'?'

'Obvious, ain't it?' grinned Mabbutt. 'That key – fits somethin', don't it? So we're goin' to find out exactly what. We take the woman with us to the bank there; we break in, and we set about findin' the lock that key turns. Anybody tries stoppin' us, well, we got the woman. Yuh with me?'

'Sure,' blinked Connors, 'but supposin' we lift ourselves a real haul, what then? We goin' to wait on Shard? He'll be here first light.'

Mabbutt spat fiercely and deliberately into the dirt. 'We lift ourselves a haul in that bank, we ride fast, the woman still along of us. Shard didn't say what he wanted us in Bedrock for, only to be here. We get paid for our services.' He spat again, 'Yeah, well, mebbe.... We get lucky and find ourselves a haul, we're away, boy, away! And Shard can go to sweet hell!'

'I'm with yuh, Duke. Right there!'

'Good, so let's go get the woman and put the rest of this godforsaken night to some decent use.'

Lawson Ridges slammed a white-knuckled fist to the table, blew a cloud of angry smoke from the cigar clenched tight in his teeth, and glared round his saloon bar as if viewing a pen of scabby-coated cattle. 'This the best we can do?' he glowered.

'Yuh got a better solution?' asked Doc Peppers quietly.

'We could get ourselves out there. Get to the bank. Stop them sonsofbitches from helpin' themselves,' flared Ridges, blowing more smoke.

'And you'll be the first to Boot Hill when it comes to buryin' Mrs Carfax, will yuh?' said Sam Berrins. 'That your idea of doin' somethin', mister – condemnin' the mayor's wife to death?'

''Course I ain't for doin' nothin' like that, just that we—'

'Anybody seen the mayor?' clipped Henry Clarke, pouring another measure of whiskey for a bruised and still dazed Casey Pike. 'Or is he just ridin' hard to save his own skin?' Nobody ventured an opinion. 'Never did trust the scumbag, anyhow,' he muttered.

'Just what the hell did that key mean, that's what I wanna know,' said Sam. 'What does it fit?'

Ridges coughed behind a spluttering of smoke. 'What's it matter?' he grunted.

'Matters a whole heap if it means them vermin are robbin' the bank!' snapped Sam.

'That's why I say we should do somethin',' persisted Ridges. 'I got money in that bank.'

'Ain't we all?' said Henry. 'But I ain't for havin' Mrs Carfax threatened worse than she is.'

'That's as mebbe,' began Ridges again. 'All I'm sayin' is—'

'A darn sight too much for my ears!' quipped Doc. 'Talkin' ain't gettin' us nowhere. My bettin' is them boys'll be clearin' town within the hour, with as much cash as they can carry. And they'll be takin' the woman with them as far as the border, anyhow. After that. . . . .'

Doc shrugged, sighed, consulted his timepiece and then the bar clock. 'Some hours yet to sun-up, so we got the time.'

'For what?' sneered Ridges.

'For gettin' ourselves organized before that fella Shard arrives. We're goin' to need horses, guns—'

'Yuh plannin' on chasin' them scumbags?' scoffed Ridges.

'Ain't you?' said Doc. 'We got to look to Mrs Carfax.'

'And what about that husband of hers?'

'He's somethin' else,' murmured Doc. 'And doubtless we'll get to him sooner or later.'

'Same as we will that plains' drifter,' added Sam thoughtfully.

'Yeah,' said Henry, 'and just where is he, f'Crissake?'

'Out there,' nodded Doc to the street beyond the batwings. 'And let's just hope he ain't sleepin'. Meantime, here's how I figure we should shape up. . . .'

Doc Peppers' plans for 'shapin' up' were sound enough – guns, horses, provisions at the ready for a speedy getaway in the tracks of Mabbutt and Connors before first light.

'Don't nobody get to any smart thinkin' of takin' them out soon as they show from the bank either,' Sheriff Berrins had added. 'They got Mrs Carfax, and they'll be usin' her as cover for clearin' town. Anybody so much as breathes outa place, and she'll be dead. I ain't havin' her blood spilled in Bedrock.

Ain't so fussed about her two-bit husband.'

Henry Clarke and Casey Pike saw things differently. 'T'ain't townsfolk bothers me,' Henry had explained, 'it's that fella totin' the Winchester. What's with him? What's he goin' to do?'

'Yeah,' Casey had offered, 'and then there's Shard ridin' in. What about him, f'Crissake?'

It had taken Mabbutt and Connors little more than a couple of hours to break into the bank and, by a process of elimination, discover that the much prized key had only one home: in the lock to the safe in Newton Carfax's office. The door had swung open with barely a squeak.

Sam Berrins and Doc Peppers had watched the bank from the opposite side of the street in a silence that had smothered their fears.

'Mebbe I could get close in there,' Sam had murmured, more to himself than to Doc. 'Slip down the back alley. Be there when them sonsofbitches step out. Mebbe I just might. . . . Two fast shots—'

'Clean through the middle of your head!' Doc had said without looking at Sam. 'Wouldn't work, and yuh know it wouldn't. If you didn't get y'self killed yuh'd only at best take out one of the rats – and still leave Mrs Carfax dead. They ain't no sorta odds. That's an execution.'

They had fallen to minutes of an uneasy, watchful silence before Sam had murmured again, 'Just don't seem right leavin' Mrs Carfax with scum like them.'

'Yeah, and try takin' her from 'em and we'd be carryin' her out already stiffening,' Doc had answered. 'Gotta face it, Sam—'

'How the hell did she get this involved, anyhow? She take the key from Newton? What was she doin' out of doors at this hour, in this situation?'

Doc probably knew the answers, but decided this was not the time to pursue them. It hardly mattered now how Amelia Carfax had come to where she found herself – assuming she was not too bewildered to recognize it. Her survival from here on was the only priority. Newton Carfax's money, as far as he was concerned, could be scattered to oblivion on the plains' wind, though he was becoming increasingly curious about the significance of the special key and just where Carfax was right now.

Lawson Ridges was packing in a hurry.

Just enough of the necessities: change of shirt, box of bullets, spare Colt, vital papers, mostly business; money, as much as he could lay his hands on without arousing suspicion – all in one saddle-bag, nothing too bulky, nothing too weighty. He guessed the others would be looking to food and water. Sufficient for as long as it took.

But how long?

Mabbutt and Connors would be well clear of town come full sun-up. Woman along of them might slow them down some, but they would dump her as soon as they felt safe.

He swallowed. Hell, who was he kidding? There would be no 'dumping': they would shoot Amelia Carfax without a second thought. Shame. She was still a good-looking woman.

Still, this was no time for getting soft-hearted. She

should have kept her nose out of her husband's business – and her hands out of his pockets! Too much at stake here. Too many risks taken to get this far. A fortune waiting. And he was going to make certain he had his share of it.

Too right! But what of Newton Carfax? Damn it, the whole scheme had been his brainchild from the outset. Only Carfax had had access to the bonds and been able to trade them without anyone questioning his authority to do so; only he had been able to store that amount of cash legitimately. Pity he had not done it a sight more safely!

But where was he now? Had he left town? Made a run for it? Would he be out there on the plains? Carfax was not the man to turn his back on money; not that amount, especially after having stolen it. And counted it!

He swallowed again as he buckled the saddle-bag and gave it a pat. These next few days were going to be difficult enough. Thoughts of Newton Carfax roaming the country at will were not—

'Yuh goin' some place?'

Ridges swung round at the sound of the voice, a sweat already beading on his brow.

'Sadie,' he smiled. 'Some night, eh? You and the girls still in one piece?'

'Oh, sure,' said the girl, folding her arms across her ample bosom as she leaned against the door jamb. 'Born survivors, ain't we? Take a sight more than gunslingin' scum to fuss us. We seen most of 'em, anyhow. More of 'em than most, come to it!'

'That's my gal!' beamed Ridges. 'Knew yuh wouldn't

let me down, especially now with all this' – he gestured to the street beyond the window of his room – 'and what's gotta be done soon as we can. Sam Berrins'll put some sorta posse t'gether, I guess. Best we can muster.'

'And yuh countin' y'self in along of 'em?'

'Why, sure I am. Need all the guns we can lay hands to if we're goin' to get Mrs Carfax outa this.'

Sadie rubbed her shoulder against the jamb. 'Mrs Carfax, eh?' she drawled. 'She who yuh really bothered about?'

'Absolutely; every last man of us. No sayin' what real state she's in, or what's waitin' on her. Gotta get her clear of Mabbutt and Connors fast as possible.'

'And the money?' frowned Sadie. 'What about all that money?'

'Money?' pouted Ridges. 'Well, I don't suppose them scum are goin' to walk outa the bank empty-handed, are they? And that key.... Well, it's gotta be for somethin'. And you can bet Mabbutt'll find it.'

'But you already know about that, don't yuh?' grinned Sadie.

Ridges' gaze tightened and narrowed. The smile faded and his face seemed suddenly darker in the faintly lit room. 'What are you sayin' there, Sadie?' he croaked.

'I think you know precisely what I'm saying. You surely don't think Carfax and me never got to *talking* during our arrangements, do you?'

Sadie pushed herself clear of the door jamb. 'Newton Carfax could be quite a talker when he'd a mind for it,' she went on, crossing to the table.

'Happy enough to talk about most things, but especially banking and money.' She ran a finger over the polished surface of the table. 'But, then, he would, wouldn't he?'

'You know, don't you?'

'He told me. 'Course he did. Damn it, I was supposed to be joining up with him and clearing town soon as you and him lifted the money. He was leaving his wife.'

Ridges wiped a hand across his brow. 'He never said nothin' about that.'

'Not exactly your business, was it?'

'So where is he now?'

'You tell me,' shrugged Sadie. 'Mebbe he's just holed up some place. Mebbe he's ridden out. All I do know is I ain't letting you outa my sight 'til the money's either lost for good or recovered.' She smiled, lifted her skirt and took a derringer revolver from her garter. 'Never go nowhere without it,' she said, levelling the aim at Ridges.

'Now hold on there, Sadie. No need for this. We got the same interests at heart. We can work t'gether.'

'Of course we can,' grinned Sadie. 'Especially the together bit, 'cus you ain't going nowhere. You're staying right here in town where I can keep an eye on you, so you can unpack that saddle-bag, mister, and pour me a drink.'

TWELVE

'How much? Hundreds, thousands? Big enough safe. Take a whole stack of money.' Sam Berrins scuffed his way over the littered floor of Newton Carfax's office to peer into the cavernous depths of the empty safe. 'Took every last cent,' he murmured to Doc Peppers, Henry Clarke and Casey Pike hovering at the back of him.

'And didn't waste no time about it either,' murmured Casey looking round the shadowed, ransacked room.

'No sign of Mrs Carfax,' said Henry, following Casey's gaze.

'No sign of anybody, that's the whole damned trouble!' scoffed the blacksmith. 'No sign of Carfax; Mabbutt and Connors and the woman gone; and not a whisper out of the fella with the Winchester. So what's with him? He finally pulled out?'

'Mebbe he's done just that,' said Sam, stepping back from the safe. 'Same as we're goin' to do. You three with me?'

'We're together,' agreed Doc. 'We ride when you're ready.'

'Ridges joinin' us?' asked Henry.

'Ain't seen him,' shrugged Sam. 'Mebbe stayin' behind to welcome Shard!'

'Let him!' grinned Henry.

'First light in an hour,' said Doc. 'Nothin' we can do here, so let's go pick up the trail while it's still fresh. North-west, I reckon.'

The four men left the bank and headed through the still night-hugged street for the livery at the far end of the town.

Mabbutt and Connors had helped themselves to a pack horse and a mount for Amelia Carfax. But more importantly to Sam's reckoning was the fact that the plains' drifter had collected his own mount and left.

He too had seemed to be heading north-west.

Lawson Ridges crossed to the door of the silent, shadowy room like a cat to a bowl of fresh cream, reached for the knob, turned it carefully, and cursed.

Damn woman had locked the door! Typical. Should have known. Sadie Shaw never left loose ends. She was a whole lot too smart, and he should have reckoned on it.

He licked his lips, rubbed his chin and crossed back to the window overlooking the street. Deserted, but not for a deal longer, he reckoned, scanning quickly to left and right. First light would be here in under the hour, and with it the sight of Sam Berrins and his posse leaving town to pick up the trail of Mabbutt and Connors.

They would not find it difficult: Mabbutt would not be overly concerned at being followed, not while ever he had Amelia Carfax along of him. She was his insurance against Berrins and his men getting too close.

The whereabouts of Newton Carfax and the plains' prowler were matters of a more worrying nature. Were they just, he mouthed to his thoughts, as he plotted how best to reach the street from the window and make it to the livery without being seen.

Easing the window open, shinning down to the boardwalk canopy and then to the street might not be so difficult: doing it as silently, as softly as a fly on a wall, and then passing unseen to Casey Pike's stables . . . that could be nerve-racking.

He thought for a moment about the money Mabbutt and Connors had lifted, and came to terms with his nerves without another twinge. He would give it a while longer to be certain that Sadie and the girls were staying quiet, then slide the window open and leave.

He could be out of town in twenty minutes.

It had taken only three minutes to open the window, a slow, soft hair's-breadth at a time, climb out to secure a foothold on the narrow ledge above the boardwalk, and tighten his grip to steady himself against the next move to the canopy.

At that moment, clinging for his life above the street, Lawson Ridges would have cut a figure of ridicule to anyone passing below who happened to spot him.

But at this hour nobody was passing.

Another tense minute and Ridges was ready to move again, this time reaching with his foot for a purchase and balance on the canopy. Tricky. Move too fast and he might slip; too slowly and the nerves began to jangle.

'Easy, easy,' he murmured to himself.

And he might have made it and been clean away to the street had it not been for the rider.

'Hell!' he hissed, steadying himself as he began to sweat at the sound of hoofbeats, the creak of leather, jangle of tack. 'Who in tarnation. . . ?'

But by then it was too late, the rider, crow-black and straight in the saddle against the first twists of light, was into the street and heading directly for the saloon.

Ridges could only wait, motionless, clinging like a fly, not daring to breathe, his gaze riveted behind the clouded sweat in his eyes on the man on the horse — and not liking one mite what he was seeing.

Fellow with a face as worn and scarred and mean-eyed as that had to be a gunslinger with few ambitions to be anything other, especially when you got to noting the size of the twin holstered guns, the rifle tight in its scabbard and blade sheathed at his back.

Two bits to sun-up that had to be Shard.

Ridges watched, the sweat turning cold on his back, his fingers hooked and numb in their grip, as the man closed on the hitching rail at the Long Spur. God willing, Sadie Shaw would stay indoors. God willing, Shard would dismount, push through the batwings and disappear.

Ridges was already praying on both counts when the man looked up.

The better part of a lifetime spent preserving himself against quick-witted, egotistic hopefuls intent on earning themselves the notoriety of being the man who shot Lucas Shard, had left the gunslinger with only one mark by which he stayed breathing: if it threatens, shoot it; you can get its name later.

One quick sight of a body clinging to a wall directly above him at a time of day when most men were still abed had been more than enough to convince Shard that the human fly was not there for his health, so he reacted instinctively and without a second thought.

His right hand drew the long-barrelled Colt from its holster and blazed two shots across the early morning that seemed to rip into the light like a honed knife-edge through taut canvas.

The first shot splintered the clapboard within a whisker of Ridges' hand and its hooked fingers. The second, blazing in its wake, was a direct hit, shattering his forearm.

Ridges yelled, groaned, felt his head begin to spin. The town roofs, street, boardwalks and mounted rider merged to a swaying blur as he lost his grip, then his balance and fell, blood flying from the wound, to the canopy below him, bounced once and continued in the momentum to crash in a heap in the dirt.

Shard, still mounted, the Colt firm in his grip, had backed his mount in a swirl of dust, his gaze shifting like a beam from Ridges, to the boardwalk, the batwings, the sight of Sadie Shaw pushing through them, then to the street.

A group of early risers, some not yet fully dressed, had wandered bleary-eyed from their homes. They stared, silent, bewildered, transfixed by the menace of Shard and the groaning, bleeding body.

Somewhere a dog howled. The Seroquoi plains' wind grew from a breeze to its familiar eerie whine.

'What's all this?' flared Sadie, bustling to the front of the boardwalk, the bar girls hovering at the batwings. She stared at Ridges, then narrowed her gaze on Lucas Shard. 'You who I think you are, mister? Lucas Shard?' she drawled, fixing her hands defiantly on her hips.

'Mornin', ma'am,' said Shard, tipping his hat as his mount backed again. 'You folk make a habit of scalin' walls?' He grinned and spat. 'S'right, ma'am, Lucas Shard in person.'

'I ain't sure you're welcome here,' glared Sadie.

'That a fact?' mouthed Shard, the grin widening.

Ridges moaned as he struggled to his knees.

'Ain't nothin' here for you, anyhow,' added Sadie. 'Your men have pulled out. Left at first light. Not before they'd emptied the bank, o'course.'

Shard's grin faded as his eyes narrowed to tight, dark slits. 'Well, now,' he murmured, 'ain't they been busy?'

'Ain't they just!' huffed Sadie, watching Ridges crawl towards her. 'Got a woman along of 'em. Mayor's wife. Sorta hostage against the sheriff's posse getting too close.' Her gaze flashed to the gunslinger.

'I'd say you're outa luck, mister.'

'Would yuh now?' sneered Shard.

' 'Course, I suppose you might catch up. Depends how hard you happen to ride.'

'Oh, don't know about that, ma'am,' said Shard, the grin settling again. 'Had me all the hard ridin' I can take for now. Time to rest up awhiles. And yuh know somethin', I'm gettin' a real fancy for this place. Especially yourself, ma'am. So I figure I might just stay. See how things pan out, eh? What yuh say?'

Shard's third shot ripped into Lawson Ridges' left leg. 'Time he broke that wall-climbin' habit!'

THIRTEEN

The four riders came abreast at the same steady pace as the morning light swept the plains and lifted the first long shadows.

Setting that pace on the far flank was Sheriff Sam Berrins, his gaze concentrated in its tightness on an horizon that had stayed empty and unbroken since the four had cleared Bedrock and headed their mounts due north-west.

Henry Clarke, his gaze similarly concentrated, rode at Sam's side. Been a while, he was reflecting, since he had been this far from town, specially so at this time of year with the wind at its whippiest. Not that he was much given to worrying about whippy winds when there was Duke Mabbutt and Nate Connors somewhere out there.

Casey Pike, a stride behind Henry, was almost certain the faint grey smudge he had seen way out to the east seconds before the full light broke had been a rider; maybe more than one if they were bunched and reined tight. Nothing to be seen now, but if the smudge had been Mabbutt, Connors and Mrs Carfax, they were closing fast on them and would be within identifiable range in another hour. How long, he wondered, before Mabbutt figured for them being close enough to be reached by a Winchester?

Doc Peppers' thoughts were back in town. He was pondering on why Lawson Ridges had seemingly disappeared, what had happened to Carfax, and what Shard would do once he discovered Mabbutt and Connors long gone. He was also troubled by thoughts of the plains' prowler.

Not much hope of him staying out of sight in these windswept lands. So would the 'wolf' get to showing himself? Would Carfax appear as if from nowhere? Would Mabbutt and Connors opt for a shoot-out first suitable chance they had, or would they hold on to the woman, increase the pace and head like the wind for the hills bordering Asparity?

Whatever, with saddle-bags of money roped to a pack horse they would grow increasingly desperate to cling to the good fortune they had stumbled across. Or had they? Why had Carfax had that amount of money locked away under his personal control? How many others knew about it? Why were types like Scully Dyke, Mabbutt and Connors tied in with Shard?

What did Shard know, or had somehow come to learn, that no one else knew? And another thing. . . .

But it was at that moment in Doc's considerations that the lone rider had broken clear and unmistakable on the distant horizon and Sam Berrins called for his party to rein up.

*

'Carfax, it's him, sure enough. Know the set of that hat any place. What the hell's he doin?' Henry Clarke squinted and leaned forward in his saddle. 'He seen us?'

'Be blind if he ain't,' grunted the blacksmith.

'We goin' to ride him down, get to the bottom of this mess?' said Henry.

'Hold on,' ordered Sam. 'Give it a minute.'

'He don't seem fussed about us,' murmured Doc, shielding his eyes against the strengthening glare. 'Seems to be concentratin' on somethin' beyond him.'

'Could be he's spotted his wife along of Mabbutt and Connors,' offered Henry.

'He gets to tanglin' with them scumbags, he'll be crow meat faster than he can—'

Doc choked on his words at the crack and echoing whine of a rifle shot that toppled Carfax from his mount like a dead weight.

Henry's mount bucked. Casey's horse pranced through a full circle. Doc Peppers groaned, gasped and blinked rapidly.

'Spread yourselves and ride!' yelled Sam, thrusting his mount to a fast gallop towards the horizon and the silhouette of the riderless horse.

'Hell, supposin—' shouted Henry on a sudden squall of wind.

'Suppose nothin'!' ordered Sam. 'Just ride!'

Doc and Casey were already veering wide to the right, Sam thrusting ahead in a near straight line, leaving Henry to complete the fan shape with his swing to the left.

They drew rapidly on the sprawled mound of the lifeless body, Sam keeping one eye beyond it on the dips and rolls of the plain for the slightest hint of the rifle shootist. Nothing obvious, but could be one or other of the gunslingers had held back among the scattered outcrops for the chance to take out Carfax.

'He's closed his account,' said Doc, squatting at the body of the banker. 'Clean shot. Wouldn't have known a thing about it.'

'Sonsof-goddamn-bitches,' groaned Henry, 'if this ain't the darnedest thing I've ever seen. What the hell we goin' to say to Mrs Carfax?'

'Got to get to her first, ain't we?' said Casey, shielding his gaze as he scanned the plains. 'Yuh see anythin', Sam? Couldn't have got that far after the shot.'

The sheriff licked his lips slowly for a moment. 'Outcrop far side of that long drift. Enough cover there for men and horses.'

'And only just out of rifle range – at the moment,' murmured Henry uncomfortably. 'Move twenty yards and we'll be sittin' targets.'

'Not if we circle to them rocks east of the drift,' said Sam.

'Risky,' grunted Henry.

'Tell that to Mrs Carfax out there,' snapped Sam.

'Talkin' ain't doin' nobody any good,' said Doc, coming upright. 'We load up this body and get it into the rocks, then we do as Sam says while we're all still standin' and breathin'. Lead on, Sheriff!'

They rode quickly at a carefully measured pace and distance, Sam Berrins leading the party through a wide arc to the huddle of the outcrop. Henry brought up the rear, trailing Carfax's mount and the body; Doc and Casey rode the flanks, their gazes tight and narrowed on the distant cover and whatever, whoever, lurked behind it.

'Well, yuh see anythin'? They there?' asked Henry, as Sam slid back to the shadows from a vantage point among the higher rocks.

'They're there,' sighed the sheriff, wiping the sweat from his neck. 'Mabbutt, Connors, Mrs Carfax. And the money.'

'So what we waitin' on?' frowned the storekeeper.

'Yuh suggestin' we charge in there like some half-wit cavalry?' sniped Casey, hitching his pants to his waist. 'We do that and they'd pick us off like flies – then shoot the woman.'

'I ain't suggestin' we do that exactly,' began Henry again. 'All I'm sayin' is—'

'We wait,' said Doc. 'Next move is theirs. That right, Sam?'

'Mrs Carfax is the problem,' mused Sam. 'Worth more than the money to them right now. And Mabbutt'll know it. So, yeah, that's it – we wait. They won't sit it out for long. Too anxious to get to the border.'

'Meantime,' said Casey, crossing to a break in the rocks to scan the sweep of the windswept plain, 'I just wonder where that prowlin' fella's gotten himself.

Yuh don't suppose he's holed up out there, do yuh?'

'Mebbe he's goin' to leave Mabbutt and Connors to us,' pondered Henry. 'Mebbe he's back in town. Could be that fella Shard's arrived. And if he has.... Hell, we still goin' to have a town?'

'Glad we've got yuh along of us, Henry,' quipped Sam. 'Yuh do enough worryin' for all of us!'

Sure he did, thought Doc, the only trouble being he just happened to be right.

FOURTEEN

Lawson Ridges sweated, groaned, winced and cursed between clenched teeth, as the bandages tightened and the blood, what little he presumed he had left, rushed to the back of his eyes.

'Do yuh have to?' he moaned, fixing his watery gaze on Sadie Shaw.

'Just lie still there, will you?' snapped the woman, with another pull on the binding on Ridges' leg. 'Think yourself lucky. This could be a whole lot worse. Shard could've finished you with that last shot. As it is' – she fastened the bandaging with a defiant grunt – 'you might live just long enough for Doc Peppers to cut the lead from this wound and do the best he can for your arm.' She stood back from the bed in the sunlit, shadow-streaked room with a sigh. 'Got to say it, Lawson Ridges, you're a mess and you look it!'

'Do yuh think I don't know, f'Crissake?'

'Tell you something else,' said Sadie, clearing the bed of its clutter and adjusting the pillows at Ridges' head, 'you ain't going no place for a long while. Best get that through your head before you start fretting on that money fast disappearing from sight.' She paused a moment. 'Not that anybody's going anywhere while Shard's here,' she added darkly.

'We gotta talk about that, Sadie,' winced Ridges. 'About the money, and about Shard. We gotta get ourselves organized.'

'Oh, sure,' mocked the woman. 'With you there and me at Shard's beck and call? Helluva lot of *organizing* we're going to get to!'

'But we gotta do somethin', damn it. Can't just let it go, can we? Where are them gunslingers now? Where's Carfax? Where's Sam Berrins and the others? And where's that prowlin' fella with the Winchester? We're talkin' a fortune at stake here, Sadie. Ain't goin' to turn our back on that, are we?'

'Aren't we?' said Sadie, moving to the door. 'Like I said, Shard could've killed you back there. You were at his mercy, and you still are. Don't forget it.' She laid a hand on the doorknob. 'So am I, come to think of it. Staying alive is going to be as much as we can hope for. And just pray that Sam and the others make it back in one piece.'

'With the money,' murmured Ridges when Sadie had left the room.

Doc Peppers squinted against the whipping edge of the plains' wind, eased his grip on his Colt and shifted his aching bones. He glanced quickly at Sam Berrins tight as a basking lizard in the rocks at his side, then at Henry and Casey sprawled among the boulders beyond him.

No one had made a sound in close on an hour.

'See anythin'?' he hissed to Sam.

'Still nothin', but that ain't goin'to last. Mabbutt'll know he's wastin' good time.' Sam wiped a hand across his mouth. 'He needs to ride.'

'Just hope Mrs Carfax ain't sufferin' too bad,' said Doc.

'She's alive, yuh can bet on that. She ain't no use dead.'

Doc grunted and squinted again. 'Wonder where the wolf's holed up?' he murmured almost to himself. 'Don't suppose—' And then he tensed behind another grunt. 'There – yuh see that?' he croaked.

'I got it,' said Sam. 'Somebody movin'. Glint of a barrel. They've hung around long enough.'

'They goin' to make a hell-for-leather break for it?' asked Henry.

'Not with that pack horse and the woman they ain't. Too risky.'

'I'd figure for them—' began Casey before the spitting, whining crack of the shot drowned his voice and buried his words.

Sam's Colt blazed instantly. Doc squinted for a target. Henry ducked.

'It's Connors!' yelled Casey. 'Mounted up and headin' straight for us!'

The gunslinger had broken clear of the rock cover in a headlong thrust of thundering hoofs, his body slung tight and low to the horse's neck, a rifle clutched to his side and already blazing wildly as he carved a weaving dash across the plain.

Sam's Colt raged, but more in instinctive retaliation than the hope of making a hit. Doc still waited for the target to close. Henry and Casey struggled to steady their hands, and nerves, as they watched Connors grow on the light like a cloud.

'He'll pass us on this side,' shouted Sam, 'and come up on the rear. Casey, you be ready at the back there. Henry, you keep one eye on them rocks. Mabbutt might try sneakin' out with the pack and the woman.' He licked his lips and furrowed his brow on a beading of sweat. 'Let's make the lead count, eh?'

Sight easier said than done, thought Doc, blinking rapidly on the thundering shape. It was as good as he could manage right now to keep Connors in focus, let alone make a hit.

The rifle fire blazed again, this time to shatter rock to flying splinters. Casey looked anxiously at the loose hitched mounts. They were getting nervy. Only needed for one of them to spook. . . .

Connors came on, his mount wide-eyed, hoofs pounding, mane flying, the rifle still steady and ripping into sudden bursts of raging lead. A shot cracked and ricocheted across the rock at Doc Peppers' shoulder, forcing him back as the splinters flew.

Sam raised himself the vital few inches that would give him a clearer view of the rider, only to drop again as another burst of shots clipped and nipped at the surfaces round him.

Henry slid from his vantage point, the sweat almost bubbling on his face. Mabbutt had made no move as yet. Maybe he would wait till Connors swung round and raced back to the outcrop, or was he hoping on one of his partner's shots getting lucky and finding a target? Way the gunslinger was pumping the lead from that rifle he had to get lucky – law of averages.

'Damn it, he keeps this up much longer and we'll all be crow meat,' spluttered Casey, gathering the reins of the restive mounts. 'Somebody give me a hand here?'

Doc stumbled to the blacksmith's side in the lull in the shooting, as Connors turned his mount and steadied it for the return dash; Henry clawed his way back to the vantage point; Sam scrambled into new cover, grabbing a Winchester from its scabbard and settling it angrily in his grip as he went.

'This time!' he croaked beneath his rasping breath. 'This time!'

Connors' mount rose on its hindlegs, its eyes white and bulging in its lathered frenzy, the man's face equally wet and wild, a grin slashed at his twisted lips as if relishing the hell-ride to come.

He raised the rifle above his head, shouted a cursed defiance and was lowering himself again to the mount's neck when the two fast shots from somewhere to his left flung him to the ground with a crashing thud.

'What in the name of—' began Sam, only to swallow on his words as a rider, dark in the saddle, was framed in a dazzle of breaking light through wind-pitched clouds.

'That's him!' croaked Henry, stumbling forward. 'That's the drifter. That's our wolf!'

'Connors ain't movin'. He's dead. Fella's shot him clean through,' murmured Casey.

Sam swung round. 'Mabbutt!' he growled. 'Watch for Mabbutt, f'Crissake. Don't let him get clear.'

'He ain't goin' nowhere neither by the look of it,' said Doc, pointing to the sweep of the open plain. 'Seems like our visitor's takin' charge.'

They watched as the man reined his mount from the body of Connors and walked it slowly towards the outcrop sheltering Mabbutt and the woman, his Winchester steady in his grip, levelled at the hip.

'Mabbutt ain't shifted a hair,' hissed Casey.

'Well, don't reckon for him bein' asleep!' clipped Henry. 'He knows the score well enough. Mebbe we should go lend a hand.'

'Does that fella look as if he needs a helpin' hand?' grunted Sam. 'Not the way I'm seein' it he don't!'

'Just who in tarnation is he?' murmured Casey. 'What's he doin' out here? Who's he doin' all this for? Could be he knows the whole story about them scumbags, and Shard. Hell, he don't seem to have a deal of time for 'em, that's for sure.'

The man had continued to move at the same measured pace, the rifle still levelled, his gaze as settled as a shaft of the light.

'When's Mabbutt goin' to move, f'Crissake?' croaked Henry.

'More to the point, what's he goin' to do about Mrs Carfax?' added Doc, squinting intently at the shape of the man as he moved steadily on.

'Duke Mabbutt could take him out easy as crackin'

a nut at that distance.' Casey licked his lips nervously. 'Don't tell me he ain't realized that.'

'You bet he has,' said Doc in little more than a whisper. 'See how he's keepin' the light behind him, that horse on a short rein. And he ain't shifted that Winchester one snitch. I'd reckon that for bein' the mark of a fella who knows—'

Doc blinked and twitched as if prodded at the suddenness of the dark bulk that rose from the rocks.

'Far enough, fella,' called Mabbutt, brandishing his twin Colts. 'I got a woman here, the mayor's wife, but I guess yuh already know that.' The man's eyes brightened like hot coals. 'Now here's the deal – and you fellas back there with the sheriff had best listen up real good too: anybody move against me when I ride outa here with my pack horse and the woman, and the woman gets it. One shot. No messin'.'

'Sonofabitch!' hissed Sam.

'Shall I take him out now, Sam?' said Casey.

'Don't even think about it. You miss, and that's it for Mrs Carfax. Too chancy. Leave it to the fella there.'

'Now I don't know who yuh are, mister,' Mabbutt called again, 'and I ain't much fussed, savin' that you've made some mess of my partner there. Should kill yuh for that by rights, but I ain't the time for it.' He stiffened. 'Yuh back off there now. I'm comin' out.'

FIFTEEN

The man sat his mount without so much as blinking. Doc swallowed and sweated. Henry simply sweated. Casey twitched once and turned cold. Sam Berrins mouthed silently, gripped the rifle and narrowed his gaze. The wind whipped through the plains' grasses. The light grew, shafted scudding shadows, shimmered.

'We ain't just goin' to stand here, are we?' croaked Henry. 'We ain't goin' to let that rat ride out. Hell, no.'

'Forget it, Henry,' said Doc. 'We're doin' nothin' 'cus that's the best we can do. Mabbutt'll shoot Mrs Carfax as easy as spittin'. And I ain't for standin' witness to that.'

They fell to a tensed, uneasy silence as they watched Mabbutt lead the pack horse and the slumped, hand-roped, bedraggled figure of Amelia Carfax from the outcrop.

'She don't look good,' hissed Casey. 'Miracle she's managin' to sit that horse. What yuh reckon, Doc?'

Doc's squint tightened. 'The miracle is she's alive at all,' he sighed. 'Let's pray we can keep it that way.'

The man's mount twitched its flanks and shifted its feet. The man rolled with the movement, his gaze still fixed, the Winchester steady and levelled. Mabbutt waited until the mounts had cleared the rocks and he had drawn the woman closer to his side before halting.

'Glad to see you fellas got some sense,' he called, his grin spreading cynically. 'Got some respect for my word, eh? Fine, that's just fine. And you might well have spared this lady here any further discomfort for a while. I'm sure she's obliged to yuh, and would say so too, savin' she's a mite weary right now, so I'll say it for her.'

The tingling in the nape of Sam Berrins's neck was an instinctive warning that something was not quite what it seemed, that what he was seeing was only a part of the picture. He had missed something.

But not for long.

The man had still not moved, or so it seemed, but now Sam noticed the softest, almost imperceptible shift of the Winchester hugged tight at his hip. Hell, he thought, conscious of the wind cooling the sweat on his brow, he was surely not going to risk . . . not from this angle, with Mrs Carfax drawn across Mabbutt like a shield. He had only Mabbutt's head as a clear target, and that for never more than seconds, so that any shot, particularly on an unsighted aim from the hip, would have to be pinpoint accurate.

Sam swallowed, glanced at the others, blinked, swallowed again on a throat suddenly as parched as plains' dust, and watched the Winchester shift the merest fraction. Now; the man would have to do it now. . . .

'So don't you fellas get to any wild thinkin', will yuh?' grinned Mabbutt, tightening the line to the pack. 'And don't try followin' neither. I spot anybody trailin' back of us—'

The shot blazed across the light like a spear of flame, the sound crashing through the whip of the wind as if sliced from it.

'What in the name of hell,' groaned Casey.

'See that,' croaked Henry. 'See that, if yuh like, damnit!'

'He's down,' shouted Doc. 'Mabbutt's down!'

'Look to Mrs Carfax, Doc,' snapped Sam, scrambling over the rocks to the open ground, his rifle tight in his grip. 'Leave the rest to—'

'He's ridin' out,' shouted Doc again. 'The wolf – he's pullin' out! What the hell's he doin' that for, f'Crissake? Stop him, can't yuh? Stop him!'

'Where's he headin'?' asked Henry, stumbling to the edge of the outcrop.

'Where do you think?' said Sam, his gaze following the shape of the disappearing rider. 'He's headin' for Bedrock. His business ain't done yet, is it?'

Sadie Shaw watched the late afternoon light begin to fade to the first shadows of evening. It had been a long, hot, windswept day, one she had figured she might be lucky to see come to a close, but she had made it this far, she thought, easing carefully across the bar of the Long Spur saloon to the batwings. She might stay lucky and see midnight and the first light of a new day. It all depended on the man seated at the table in the corner.

'Yuh ain't thinkin' of goin' for a stroll, I hope,' drawled Lucas Shard, idling a deck of cards through his fingers. 'Could be a whole lot unhealthy out there.'

'Me?' frowned Sadie, a playful grin at her lips. 'Now would I do such a thing at this time of day? A lady don't venture out of doors come evening, save when escorted, and I can see you ain't going no place.' She reached the 'wings and gazed over the silent, deserted street where even the wind seemed a stray. 'We waiting on something? Or maybe somebody?' she asked lightly.

'Could be we are doin' just that,' said Shard, his concentration on the cards.

'Well, now,' quipped Sadie, 'let's just figure for who that might be. Hardly likely we're going to see them scumbags, Mabbutt and Connors, again, is it? Can't hardly see them bringing the bank's money back, can you?'

Shard raised his eyes but stayed silent.

'So,' continued Sadie, still gazing over the street, 'you could be reckoning on Carfax showing up, but I figure for him staying on the trail of his money. Wherever that is, is where you'll find Carfax – unless, of course, somebody decides he's making a nuisance of himself.'

Sadie glanced quickly at Shard, then returned to watching the steadily darkening street. 'Meantime, there's Sheriff Berrins and Doc Peppers and the others, ain't there?' she went on. 'Where are they? What are they doing? Supposing they've caught up with Mabbutt and his sidekick. What then? Or supposing. . . .' She grimaced. 'Best not do too much supposing, had we? Gets dangerous.'

Shard dealt the cards carefully to himself.

'But, of course,' said Sadie on a long, despairing sigh, 'the real nub of it all is the prowling stranger, ain't it? He's the danger in all the supposing, because we don't know who he is, what he is, where he is, or when he might show next, do we?' She turned from the 'wings to stare at Shard. 'What do you figure on that score, mister? You must have an opinion.'

Shard laid aside the cards and leaned back, his hands flat on the table. 'Ain't exactly short of opinions yourself, are yuh? Plenty of lip there, lady. So mebbe you should tell me about the mysterious prowlin' man.'

'Oh, sure,' mocked Sadie, flouncing provocatively across the room to lean on the bar. 'Sure. Big partner of mine, ain't he? Mister, I don't know any more about him than the rest, save that I'd bet a boot to a tin mug he shot Scully Dyke, that he's already caught up with Mabbutt and Connors, and that he knows you and knew you were coming here.'

Sadie pushed herself clear of the bar and strolled back to the batwings. 'Question now, of course, is: will he return to Bedrock? And if he does, I'd reckon for him being here for only one reason, wouldn't you?'

Shard came slowly to his feet, his gaze like a glaze

of ice on the woman's face. 'You tell me, lady,' he growled.

Sadie could have given him a very real answer. She had seen it there in the street only seconds ago. The softest shift of a shape through the shadows, but no mistaking it for a man, and definitely no mistaking the Winchester tight in his hand.

As it was, Sadie's answer was simple enough: 'Maybe we'll have to wait and see,' she said, turning her back deliberately on the wind-whipped street.

'She said anythin'?' asked Sam Berrins, easing to Doc's side to gaze at the woman sprawled on the ground in the shelter of the rocks. 'She don't look good.'

'Shock and a state of exhaustion,' said Doc, watching the flickerings of troubled breathing at Amelia Carfax's lips. 'She'll be fine, though how she's goin' to take the death of that husband of hers, Lord above knows.'

'She knew about him and Sadie, must have, but as for the money – hell, don't figure that for myself. But tell yuh somethin', that prowlin' fella sure does.'

'And speakin' of him,' began Doc, 'we should be gettin' back on the trail, hit town by midnight if we're lucky.'

'Ain't no sayin' to what we're goin' to find there,' said Henry, joining the sheriff. 'Still, we got the money. Mebbe we'll stand for some sorta reward.'

'We cartin' all the bodies back?' asked Casey. 'Mrs Carfax'll want her husband buried decent, but as for

Mabbutt and Connors.... I'd as soon as leave 'em for crow meat.'

'They all come back,' said Sam. 'Load 'em up now. We pull out in an hour.'

Casey and Henry moved away to the mounts. Sam pushed his hat from his brow, wiped the sweat clear and scanned the far horizon. 'Know somethin', Doc,' he murmured, 'tell yuh straight up, I ain't never seen shootin' like that fella showed there. Never. So just who in tarnation gets to learnin' to handle a piece like that? Who, f'Crissake?' He scratched his head.

'Makes the outlook interestin', don't it?' smiled Doc. 'Especially if Shard's decided to pay us a visit.'

SIXTEEN

Sadie Shaw crossed her fingers, bit nervously at her bottom lip and prayed silently beneath her breath that she would make it across the street to the shadowed boardwalk opposite.

She was mad, of course. Had to be to leave the comparative safety of the saloon, where all she had to handle was the brooding Lucas Shard, and risk her neck like this, chasing a shadow she had about as much chance of catching as she had of ever wearing a law badge.

But it was worth the try.

The prowling fellow was in town – that much she could vouch for – and was probably planning on working alone in the way he seemed to prefer, but if Shard was to be his target a helping hand on the 'inside' was not going to come amiss, especially if he was looking to gain entry unseen to the Long Spur. There were ways.

And besides, she thought, clenching her fingers

anxiously, things around Bedrock had changed, and not for the better. She had probably seen the last of Newton Carfax, almost certainly said goodbye to any of his promised money, trusted Ridges with all the faith she would put in playing with a rattler, and could not look Shard in the eyes without seeing death writ bold and black.

No, she had decided earlier, changing into pants, boots and shirt and slipping quietly out the back way at the saloon while Shard dozed fitfully at the corner table, Bedrock was going to look a whole lot healthier out of sight.

She would try to find the prowler and offer her help. Take it or leave it, she would saddle up fast as she could and leave town in what she stood in. Ride through the night; reach Asparity by noon tomorrow, then head west.

With the man back in town, she could only guess that Sam Berrins and his party had caught up with Mabbutt and Connors out there on the plain. Well, no time to wait on the outcome of that or the fate of the luckless Carfax. Shame, though, she would not have the opportunity of telling his wife a few home truths.

She shivered in the chill of the sneaking night wind, took a last look round her and crossed the street.

So far, so good, she thought, heading for the livery.

Damn the woman! She was out, right there in the street, making a run for it! He might have known, should have figured it. Tart by trade and tart by nature.

Lawson Ridges groaned, screwed his eyes tight, clenched his teeth and gripped his bandaged leg against the stabbing pain as he hobbled from the window back to the bed and fell across it like a beached whale.

Come the day he got his hands on Sadie Shaw he would personally.... Who the heck was he kidding, he thought, his gaze fixed on the shadow-streaked ceiling. He was never going to see the woman again. She was getting out while she had the chance. And could he blame her? Hardly.

Carfax and the promise of a new future for her had been blown to the wilderness somewhere out there on the Seroquoi plains. The man and the money were gone – a fact he was fast pushing himself to realize.

Bedrock offered only a deadly web of darkness with Lucas Shard currently brooding at the heart of it. This was no place to be, not for Sadie Shaw or anybody else who set any store by staying alive. And that included himself.

He struggled to sit upright on the edge of the bed, wiped the lathering of sweat from his face and neck, blinked, and licked his parched, swollen lips. If Sadie Shaw could make it out of town, so could he. He would have to, damn it. No saying when Sam Berrins, Doc and the others would return, if they ever did.

And there was a way. Risky, difficult, but a way, assuming he could get out of the room and find the strength – and be lucky enough – to reach his office.

Once there, well, things might change for the better.

He winced again and came unsteadily to his feet.

Sadie was moving, quickly now, slipping smoothly, silently through the shadows, her knowledge of every foot, every creaking timber of the boardwalk, the alleys between buildings to be avoided, the stretches of darkness to be exploited, giving her an edge that overcame her natural fear and calmed her jangling nerves.

The town was still quiet, most folk judging it the saner part of courage to stay indoors. Faint lights flickered in shaded windows; a hound scurried for cover at the approach of steps; venturesome vermin welcomed the silence and stillness and hunted almost nonchalantly; an owl hooted and swept in low and easy from the plain, the still brisk wind setting it to a skimming drift over the bent grasses.

Sadie paused to catch her breath, the livery within reach in her next dash. If the prowling man was anywhere, she figured, it had to be the livery. He would have looked to his mount and doubtless reckoned for the stabling being a safe refuge until at least first light.

But when, she wondered, did he plan to make a move against Shard? Would he wait on Sam Berrins returning? What had happened out there on the plain? When would Shard move? How long had she got before he realized she had gone?

'Hell!' she hissed softly as the questions spun like lights through her head. 'Forget it,' she added. 'Do it!'

She stepped softly from shadow to shadow, paused again, anxious now to make the crossing from the last of the boardwalk to the cluttered sprawl of the livery, forge and Casey Pike's shack.

She would head for the deepest darkness at the forge, she decided, then from there to the cover of the piled timbers at the corral. Only a matter of yards then to the stabling. And if the man was hidden there. . . .

He might have been; could even have been aware of her, watching, waiting for her to cross to the forge, but, like Sadie, he would have been forced to step back in the next moments at the slow scuffing of hoofs through dirt, the creak of tired leather, soft jangle of tack.

Riders, two of them, dark in stark silhouette in the scudding of moonlight, moving at an even pace, the horses short reined, the men watchful as if expecting any one of the shadows surrounding them to spring into life.

Sadie tensed against a cold shiver, swallowed, her eyes wide on the approaching riders. Not Sam Berrins and Doc, nor any one she knew or had seen before. Strangers, from out of town, and no mistaking now as they rode closer and passed through a glow of light, the look of them.

Gunslingers if ever she had seen the likes – and she had, more times than she cared to recall or could count.

Only one reason they had discovered Bedrock at this hour, she decided; only one place they were heading, only one man they were here to meet.

They were Shard's men.

Not surprising he had been in no hurry to leave town, content to sit it out at the corner table. 'Hell,' she hissed again, backing deeper into the boardwalk shadows. What now? Could she still make it to the livery? Would her best plan be to get out of town as fast as she could, leaving the prowler to his own devices?

The riders had drawn level, were moving on still at the same slow pace to the same scuff of hoofs, creak of leather. She would wait till they were closer to the saloon, then make her dash to the forge. No messing; if she could find a horse, saddle it up. . . .

The riders had halted, their backs to the boardwalk, and were just sitting there, silent, staring into the empty street.

'Know somethin'', said the rider on the left nearest the walk, 'I smell a woman. I surely do. Now just what do you suppose a woman would be doin' out here this time of night?'

When he reined his mount round the man seemed to Sadie to be staring directly into her eyes.

Seconds later she knew he was.

SEVENTEEN

Lawson Ridges reached the next sprawl of deep shadow and slid into it like a tired lizard looking for somewhere to sleep. He tensed, took a deep breath against the stabbing pains in his leg, wiped the sweat from his face and stared into the shadows still to come.

Another dozen yards and he would be at the door to his office at the end of the corridor that ran the length of the rear of the Long Spur saloon. It would be locked, as it always was.

But he had the key.

He smiled softly to himself. In other words, he thought, trying his best to disregard the pain, in approximately thirty minutes he would have a gun in his hand, money in his pocket and every chance of being clear of Bedrock before first light.

Providing his luck held.

He grunted at the necessity for the proviso, but he was nothing if not a realist. Only luck was finally going to pull this off, and he knew it.

He waited, listened, peered into what he could see of the dimly lit, deserted saloon bar below him. He could see nothing of Lucas Shard, so could only assume he was either dozing or had gone in search of Sadie. The town was sleeping, even the late customers and drunks were long abed, and the bar girls had taken refuge in their rooms here on the first floor.

All was quiet, all was still. A fellow needed a slice of that sort of luck from time to time.

He took another deep breath and moved slowly on, conscious of the injured leg beginning to drag, the boot to scuff at the floorboards. He winced as if to summon silence and blinked on a surge of cold, clinging sweat.

Another sprawl of deep shadow, another few feet nearer to the office door. He paused again, waited, listened, watched. The silence held, the night remained still and empty.

He was about to shuffle on, passing a door only inches from his face, when it creaked open and two intensely blue, round and astonished eyes stared into his.

'Mr Ridges!' hissed the girl, struggling self-consciously to hide her state of undress.

Ridges sighed, closed his eyes and pressed a finger to his lips.

'What are you doing?' hissed the girl again through the narrowest crack between door and jamb. 'You shouldn't be on your feet. Sadie said—'

'Sadie ain't here,' croaked Ridges. 'She's pulled out. Gone. Left town.'

The girl blinked and gasped. 'What about that man – Shard? Where's he?'

'Ain't seen him. Look, will yuh just close that door, stay outa sight. I got to—'

There was the sound from the bar of a chair being pushed back, heavy footfalls across the room to the batwings, and then the sight of Shard staring into the night.

'Quick, in here, Mr Ridges,' said the girl opening the door wider as she grabbed at Ridges' arm.

'No. I—'

But then it was too late and he was into the room, the door closed and locked behind him, the pain in his leg throbbing wildly and the girl searching madly for her clothes.

Sadie Shaw gulped and retched at the smell of the man seated behind her on the slow stepping mount.

She was going to be sick, sure of it, even though there were no more than a few yards to go to the boardwalk fronting the saloon. The smell, the closeness of the trail-scuffed, dirt-stained gunslinger. . . .

She gulped again. His equally stained and dirt-mouldy partner with the matted ginger beard riding at their side was as bad, if not worse.

'She ain't much for talkin', is she?' leered ginger beard, reaching to run a hand down Sadie's thigh. 'Nice filly, though,' he grinned. 'Didn't figure on no bonus this shape.'

'Don't yuh go assumin' nothin',' mouthed the man's partner. 'Woman ain't yours yet.' He spat over Sadie's shoulder to the dirt. 'I found her, I keep her.'

Ginger beard smiled and shrugged. 'Shard might say otherwise. Mebbe he already knows her. Mebbe she's some classy whore. Looks it.'

Sadie stiffened and closed her eyes.

'Shard can say and do as he pleases where money's concerned: women are different; women are mine.'

'Share and share alike, big Brother,' sneered ginger beard. 'Just like we always do. Bedrock ain't no place to go changin' things.' He reached for Sadie's thigh again. 'Shame we didn't find her sooner.' He reined his mount tight. 'Saloon comin' up, and lo and behold I do believe our good friend Mr Shard is waitin' up on us there. Ain't that obligin? Yeah, real obligin' place, ain't it, Brother?'

'We just ridin' in? Bodies, money and all. Yuh figure that for bein' safe?' Doc Peppers glanced quickly at Sam Berrins mounted alongside him on the moonlit plains' trail. 'Could slip in the back way.'

'Or wait on first light,' said Henry Clarke from behind them. 'Depends whose been wipin' their boots at our backdoor, don't it?'

'Shard for certain,' offered Casey.

'One gun against the rest of us?' said Henry. 'Us *and* the wolf, assumin' he's up there ahead of us.'

'He's there,' murmured Sam, 'Yuh can bet on that.' He drew his reins tighter to one hand and checked anxiously on the woman trailing silent and still dazed at his side. 'You hold in there, ma'am,' he soothed. 'Soon have yuh home and safe in your bed.'

Amelia Carfax's smiled response was thin and wan as she struggled against a shiver and glanced hurriedly at the dead bodies being trailed by Casey Pike and Henry.

'Don't torment yourself,' soothed Sam again. 'Ain't nothin' to be done about that, ma'am. We'll fathom it all later. Meantime, town's comin' up. Yuh goin' to be able to cope?' She nodded, sniffed and stared fixedly into the night. 'We'll go in the back way like Doc suggests.'

'I'll be there for yuh, ma'am, don't you fret none,' smiled Doc. 'Been a rough time for all of us.'

Doc grunted and bit back any further comment he might have made. Amelia Carfax was maybe as uncertain as the others on what awaited once they left the trail for Bedrock.

'Just keep yuh eyes well skinned,' said Sam quietly, narrowing his gaze on the dark shapes of the town in the distance. 'And everybody, keep it real quiet. Any luck at all and we might make it without the whole town turnin' out.'

But the whole town turning out might be just what they needed most, thought Doc. That way they might stay safe.

Or had Lucas Shard ever been that self-conscious? He doubted it.

'Sadie ain't goin' no place,' clipped the girl through clenched teeth, as she slipped back to the room, wincing at the click of the door behind her. 'I just seen her, down there, in the bar.'

She stared moon-eyed and glistening under a glow of fresh sweat at Lawson Ridges perched nervously at the foot of her bed.

'Yuh sure?' said Ridges.

'Certain. There's two fellas with her as well as Shard.'

'Yuh recognize them?'

'Sure I do,' frowned the girl, wiping the sweat from her face. 'Seen 'em when I was at the Palace out Dead Rocks. And they weren't good news then neither.' She crossed to the window and peered into the empty, silent, moonlit street. 'Trail-stinkin' scum of the worst kind.' She scanned to left and right, then turned in a flash of skirt and bobbing hair. 'Yuh say yuh were on your way to your office when I heard yuh and opened the door. That so?'

'Yes,' said Ridges hesitantly. 'But—'

'Why?' snapped the girl. 'What were yuh after? A gun by any chance?'

'Well. . . .'

'A gun. Right, I'll go get it.'

'Now wait a minute—' began Ridges.

'There ain't the time. Just tell me where it is. You may not be fussed about stayin' alive, but I sure as hell am!'

EIGHTEEN

Liam O'Leary and his ginger-bearded younger brother, Scats; about as deadly and miserable a combination you would cross this side of Banister's Canyon. And they had to be here, in Bedrock!

Sadie winced and tried to bring her tousled hair into shape as she watched Shard greet his new recruits with a fresh bottle of Long Spur whiskey. Scraping in the real mire of the barrel with this pair, she thought, easing closer to the window at her side. The O'Leary brothers were about the last to trust with anything, anywhere, anytime.

So if Shard was figuring for these two being fit to rub their grubby fingers over a big haul of money, he had best think again. And be real careful when he got to telling them the prize had already been lifted!

'Took a while longer to get here than we'd planned,' the elder O'Leary was saying, sinking his third shot of whiskey. 'The others here? We all set to make a move?'

'Sure, anytime now,' answered Shard, his glance

flicking quickly to Sadie. 'Town's in my lap, savin' for a rogue gun I got prowlin'.'

'Lead me to it,' leered Scats. 'I ain't had m'self a decent shootin' since that day out the Pearson spread. You hear about that?'

'And he don't want to neither,' clipped Liam. 'Not now. We got other matters to discuss. Big money for a start.'

'Sure,' began Shard again. 'Have yourselves a seat here and I'll put yuh in the picture....'

This is where things could start to get tricky, thought Sadie, straining to peer through the window as the three men took their seats at the table. Not a deal to see save the dark, shadowy blur of the street, the black bulks of the buildings. No sounds. Nothing moving.

She turned away, conscious for a moment of a fleeting movement above her, somewhere at the head of the stairs; a person, somebody moving slowly, carefully. Surely not Ridges, she frowned. One of the girls? Just the sort of crazy caper Patsy would get up to given half the chance.

'What yuh sayin' there?' growled Liam O'Leary, his face tense, wet with sweat. 'I hearin' yuh right? The money's gone?'

'Just hear me through here, will yuh?' protested Shard. 'Yuh gotta see the whole picture first.'

'I'm seein' one helluva picture,' hissed Scats, his hands flat on the table. 'And I don't like what I'm seein' one bit. Not at all, Mr Shard. What yuh reckon, big Brother? We got some decidin' to do.'

Shard came watchfully to his feet. 'Now yuh hold

up there, pair of yuh. Just remember who put this whole thing together. Hadn't been for me yuh wouldn't none of yuh known of Newton Carfax and his plan to rob his own bank through the cashin' of other folks' bonds. Hadn't been for him approachin' me in Asparity as the gun who would take out Lawson Ridges when the time came, you pair wouldn't be within a hundred miles of Bedrock.'

Sadie swallowed. Hell, this was a side of the plotting she had not been told. Somebody maybe did Ridges a favour when they put him out of action. She glanced quickly to the shadows at the head of the stairs. All still, all quiet. She swallowed again and stared at Shard.

'Now I got Ridges right here, under this roof,' the gunslinger went on, hooking this thumbs to his belt, 'and he ain't in no state to do anythin' or go anywhere. I seen to that, so he's out of the picture.'

'So's Scully Dyke,' sneered Scats.

'Knowin' Scully,' quipped Shard, 'I'd reckon for him bringin' his demise on his own head. Ask the woman there; she'll tell yuh.'

Sadie stiffened and stared, but stayed silent and unmoving.

'What about Mabbutt and Connors?' said Liam O'Leary, leaning forward, his elbows tight on the table. 'I known them for years. Rode t'gether on the Silverstown job.'

'Greed,' snapped Shard on a soft grin. 'Just that – greed. Couldn't wait on us gettin' here! Got lucky, found Carfax's haul and robbed us – and themselves!'

'Yuh sayin' that's the last we seen of the money?' mouthed Scats, licking on his sweating top lip.

' 'Course I ain't,' smiled Shard. 'Think I'd still be here if I thought that? What's with you fellas? Yuh plain dumb or somethin'?'

'Yuh hold on there, mister—' mumbled Scats.

'That money'll be back here in Bedrock before sun-up,' announced Shard defiantly.

'Yuh sound awful sure about that,' said Liam, his eyes narrowing. 'How come?'

'Figure it,' smiled Shard again, walking away from the table to the bar. 'Mabbutt and Connors will almost certainly head for the border, and at no great rate at that with a pack and the woman in tow. Border's about the extent of their thinkin'. Sheriff and his posse will catch up in no time.'

'But that ain't no guarantee—' began Liam.

'Yuh right, O'Leary, it ain't.' Shard examined his long fingers. 'But the fella who's been prowlin' round town with an itchy finger on a Winchester assuredly is.'

'Yuh know him?' frowned Scats.

Sadie stiffened, her breath like a rock in her throat.

Shard lowered his hands to his sides. 'I know him,' he murmured, staring into space. 'I seem to have known him all my life – like a hauntin'.'

The O'Leary brothers gazed at Shard without a sound escaping them. Sadie waited, watching, a part of her concentration on the gunslinger broken by the shadows at the top of the stairs where still nothing moved.

Shard walked slowly along the sprawl of the bar, one finger tracing its edge as he went. 'Unless I'm much mistaken,' he said quietly, 'the fella lurkin' here in Bedrock, who seems to have been around some time, who yuh can bet yuh sweet life shot Scully Dyke, is one by the name of Drew — Marshal John Drew. Yuh heard of him?'

'He outa San Moines?' croaked Liam.

'The same,' nodded Shard.

'But he called it a day a year or more back. Leastways, he left San Moines.'

'He did that, sure enough,' said Shard. 'Retired. And yuh know for why?'

The O'Learys stared, Scats' mouth dropping steadily open.

'He retired to set himself the single task of trailin' me 'til the day would dawn when he could kill me.' Shard smiled. 'He's gettin' close, ain't he?'

Sadie stifled a shiver that crept like a cold-footed lizard over her spine.

'Yuh can't be certain it's John Drew out there, can yuh?' said Liam, shifting his stained bulk uncomfortably. 'Any case, yuh did your time back at Kee Mounts. Heard as how yuh did. And another thing, even if you are right, how come he got to hear about Bedrock? Who told him about Carfax?'

'That I don't know. But he heard — and he's here.' Shard helped himself from a bottle on the bar. 'Here now. This very night.'

'So what's so special about you?' grunted Scats. 'How come a fella throws in his badge to track one fella? Yuh ain't got no price on yuh head worth that much. This somethin' personal?'

'I guess yuh could say that,' murmured Shard, staring into the night beyond the batwings. 'Yeah, yuh'd say that – personal. I shot Drew's wife.'

The lizard on Sadie's spine crept on unchecked.

Liam O'Leary's eyes bulged like white stones in black mud.

'Hell's teeth,' croaked Scats. 'Did yuh have to?'

Shard glowered and spat into the spittoon at the end of the bar.

'So what we goin' to do, big Brother?' asked Scats. 'We gettin' outa this mess while we got the chance? There ain't no money. We don't know for sure there ever will be, and we got a crazed one-time marshal lead-happy for a killin'. I ain't for gettin' caught in no crossfire, yuh hear? Not no way, not when it ain't our fight.'

'Yuh sit tight there, pair of yuh,' growled Shard, a Colt suddenly firm and levelled in his hand. 'Ain't nobody goin' no place.'

Sadie wiped cold sweat from her eyes and blinked sharply at the movement, a blurred shape now, across the shadows on the stairs.

'We might have to get to lookin' at that a mite closer,' began Liam, but got no further with either the looking or discussing, as the stairs and bar erupted under a hail of wild, flying lead.

NINETEEN

Sheriff Sam Berrins and his party were within a dozen strides of turning to sneak into Bedrock by the little-used back trail, when the crack, roar and whine of gunfire, the splintering of broken glass and a woman's terrified screams ripped across the darkness and echoed on the chill plains' wind.

'What the hell?' croaked Henry.

'Shard,' was the only word on Casey Pike's lips.

'Saloon,' grunted Doc, reining quickly to Amelia Carfax's side. 'Yuh goin' in?'

'No choice,' said Sam, swinging his mount to the main street. 'Get Mrs Carfax safe and stow these bodies some place,' he ordered. 'Casey, you get the money hidden in the livery. Doc, yuh'd best stand along of me. I got a feelin' yuh might be needed down there.'

Seconds later the party had broken up and Sam and Doc were easing their mounts slowly down the main street to the pale, pinched lantern-light at the saloon where now there was only the drift of gunsmoke curling over the batwings.

Scat's O'Leary grabbed the bar girl, twisted her arm into her back, kicked aside the Colt she had emptied and wiped the barrel of his own gun across her neck. 'You want I should kill her now?' he sneered.

'Leave her,' growled Shard. 'That scumbag, Ridges, put her up to this. Yuh wanna go for a killin', kill him. Upstairs some place.'

O'Leary pushed the girl aside and into Sadie's waiting reach.

Liam spat violently, growled and crossed to the batwings where he scanned the street like a hawk watching for a hint of supper.

'We got company,' he announced, already feeling for the butt of his Colt.

'Who?' asked his brother striding to his side.

'Sheriff Berrins for one,' said Shard lightly. 'Almost on time. He trailin' any packs?'

'Nothin',' grunted Scats. 'Just him and an older fella.'

'Go welcome 'em then,' snapped Shard. 'Pannin' out just like I said, ain't it? Yuh still pullin' out?'

Liam spat again and pushed open the batwings, his brother stepping in his shadow.

Sadie eased the still trembling bar girl to a chair, settled her and glanced anxiously back to the shadows at the top of the stairs. No sign of Ridges, nothing of the other girls. She swallowed. And nothing of John Drew. Not yet.

Sadie eased away again, this time to the side of the

'wings. Hell, she thought, her gaze already wet and stinging as she watched the street, the O'Learys could take out Sam and Doc Peppers with just two shots if they were of a mind.

When had they ever not been of a mind?

'Now you just take it easy there, Mrs Carfax,' said Henry Clarke, ushering the woman to the cushioned depths of an easy chair in the back room parlour of his store. 'You're safe now and there ain't goin' to be no more killin's and blood and all that.' He grinned thinly, his hands shaking and fluttering over her as she collapsed with a sigh and closed her eyes.

'That's it, ma'am, real easy,' he added, backing slowly to the door to the store. 'I'm goin' to be right here for you. Right there in the store, so yuh only gotta call if yuh need me. Just need to give an eye to Sam and Doc, just in case they need me out there in the street. Not that they will, o'course. Nossir. We're soon goin' to have this town back to somethin' like. You just bet on it, ma'am. So yuh take it easy like I say. You're still in a state of shock there, but Doc'll have yuh right in no time. You see if he don't.'

Henry slid away to the dark, shadowed depths of the store, to a spot between a pile of blankets and a box of axe handles and besoms at the window.

'Hell's teeth,' he murmured to himself, lowering his bulk to the shadows, 'who in heck am I kiddin'? Just see that out there.'

He squinted and peered closer as the batwings at the Long Spur swung open and two men swaggered to the boardwalk. 'Who the devil . . .' he hissed, shifting his gaze to the approaching shapes of Sam and Doc.

Too late now for the sheriff to change plan or direction; too late to do anything save keep coming. Henry swallowed, squinted again. There was a third man, just behind the wings. Had to be Shard. And there, damn it, a brief glimpse of Sadie Shaw! So where was Ridges?

Goddamn it, just how many guns were there in Bedrock? Not surprising folk were keeping out of sight.

Maybe he should get out there, rouse Casey at the livery. Better still, he should maybe get to looking for the plains' wolf. Where the devil was he?

He twitched at a sound from the parlour, glanced anxiously towards it, half expecting to see Mrs Carfax on her feet, began to come fully upright and ducked again at the sudden searing sheet of flame leaping from the window of an upstairs room at the saloon.

Henry winced, ducked lower, fell against the besoms on the rumbling roar of a fireball explosion. 'Hell!' he groaned, his head filling now with the pitched screams of bar girls, the eerie creak and splinter of burning timber, the crash of something that spiralled a shower of sparks high into the night sky.

He heard Amelia Carfax groaning and staggering to her feet, turned and scurried back to the parlour at almost the same moment as the shadowed shape of a man, a Winchester in his grip, slid from the rear of the saloon and headed into the street.

*

Casey Pike had barely finished unloading the panniers of money and stacking them safely in the deepest recesses of the livery when the sky exploded and began to bleed.

He had rushed from the stabling, through the forge to the street just as Doc Peppers and Sheriff Sam Berrins were bringing their prancing, bucking mounts under control and struggling to hitch them at the rail fronting the funeral parlour.

'Sonofa-goddamn-bitch,' he had muttered in an already bone-dry throat and rushed back to the forge in search of his rifle.

'What the hell's happenin'?' groaned Doc, finally managing to hitch his mount and join Sam on the shadowed boardwalk. 'Who's doin' is the torchin', f'Crissake?'

'Ridges, the prowler, one of the gals . . . might be anybody,' murmured Sam. 'But it ain't Shard, that's for certain.'

'And it ain't either of them,' said Doc, pointing to the men gathering on the street fronting the saloon. 'Yuh see who we got in town? The O'Learys. Damnit, place's becomin' a trash bin!'

Sam took a grip on his rifle. 'Stay close, Doc, and keep me covered,' he snapped, blinking on the steadily thickening smoke as the flames took hold and the Long Spur began to crumble.

'Hell, Sam,' coughed Doc, 'we get the plains' wind blowin' any stronger than it is and the whole town'll go up!'

Sam wiped his eyes. 'I know, I know, but I gotta get to them scumbags back there first. We don't rid ourselves of them there won't be a town worth havin', anyway. Cover me – and try keepin' the townfolk clear of the guns.' He wiped his eyes again. 'Find Casey. Get him to organize puttin' that damned fire out! Let's go!'

Sam and Doc moved away like morsels of shadow to be swallowed by the billowing smoke.

Sadie had sprung into life at the first rush of flame.

No point in wondering how the fire had started or whose hand had been behind the torching – it hardly mattered now, she figured, with a quick glance at the lick of flame already threatening the stairs.

'Shift yuh butts, gals!' she had yelled at the top of her voice. 'Scatter fast as yuh can if yuh want to stay breathin'!'

Liam O'Leary had made to grab her, missed and thought better of a second try as Shard barked his orders.

'Get yuh hands off the woman and round the neck of that sheriff if you're still lookin' to a payout. And watch for Drew!'

Sadie had counted the bar girls clear of the stairs like a mother hen ushering her brood to safety.

'Where's Ridges?' she had spluttered, fanning her arms against the smoke.

'My room,' blubbed Patsy, blowing her nose. 'Leastways he was.'

'He ain't now,' shouted a girl, clearing the stairs in a flurry of petticoats. 'There ain't nobody up there. Not living, anyhow.'

'Damn,' mouthed Sadie. But too late now. Forget

him. 'Here we go, gals,' she yelled. 'Hit the street and keep goin' 'til yuh feel safe. We'll regroup later.' Assuming, she thought, there would be a later.

She left the burning bar that had been her home and way of life for more years than she cared to recall without so much as a second glance.

And not a dollar to her name.

TWENTY

Lawson Ridges had somehow crawled, slithered, scrambled his way from the bar-girl's room at the first crack of gunfire on the stairs.

The trail of blood he had left in his wake, as clear as the smear of a travelling snail, had been telltale enough, but what the hell, he had figured? He was either going to bleed to death or get shot in the attempt to find Doc Peppers. And being a saloon keeper he reckoned on one last gamble being worth the effort.

The place being set alight had not been an option in the odds.

He had reached the door to the outside stairs at the back of the saloon, one hand reaching for the knob, when it had opened and a man, tall, in dark clothing, his hat set low on his brow, a Winchester firm in his grip, had stepped over him with no more than a fleeting glance as if avoiding street dirt.

Ridges' voice had croaked on words that would not form in the gasping strain of movement, and the man – almost certainly the prowling drifter, he reckoned – had slid away among the shadows in the corridor without a sound.

Ridges had struggled on, through the now open door to the stairs, dark and perilous in the night light when the only way of negotiating them was by painful slide and slither.

He had given only scant thought to the man. Did he have a choice? None. His only concern was to reach the street and call, if he could find the voice, for help.

The first flash of flame, the sudden showers of sparks, the ball of heat that seemed to rush at him as if spat by the wind, had been almost enough to send Ridges crashing from his slender hold on the stairs.

'Sonofan-almighty-bitch!' he had moaned between keeping his balance, wincing against the pain in his leg and the clinging icy chill of the sweat that lathered him.

'What the hell yuh doin' there?' he had finally managed to croak. 'Yuh gone plumb crazy? Hey, you in there, whoever yuh are. . . .'

The flames had grown, climbing higher from the first floor to the roof to lick like tongues at the beams; screams pierced the whine of the wind, sounds of confusion, shouts, the thud of boots, crashing of doors and windows filled the night until it seemed to Ridges that not only had he been tossed into nightmare, but was being held down to witness every last gruesome horror of it played out in front of him.

His voice had failed again, his eyes bulged to

bloodshot coals when the man reappeared at the top of the stairs, grabbed him by the collar and bundled, dragged and bounced him to the alley, then to within feet of the street, his screams of agony lost in the throb of the mayhem.

'Shame about yuh saloon,' the man had said, staring like a black-eyed hawk into Ridges' pain-creased face, 'but yuh should've thought about that day yuh got involved in all of this.' He had spat carefully into the dirt. 'Yuh friend Carfax is dead, case you're interested, and the money's back here. T'ain't goin' no other place 'til it's returned to its rightful owners.' He glanced quickly into the street, squinting against the glow of the leaping flames. 'I guess somebody'll find yuh eventually. I'll bid yuh goodnight.'

'Who the hell are yuh, mister?' Ridges gasped.

The man had paused on the edge of the shadows, turned and looked back with the flames of the fire mirrored in his stare. 'You'll get to hear one of these days,' was all he said.

And then the night claimed him.

Sam Berrins dodged into the depths of the shadows and the cover of the boardwalk as the bar girls spilled from the saloon, Sadie Shaw waving her arms in their wake as if clucking her nestlings into brush, driving them through the gunslingers and dazed onlookers with barely a glance.

He called to her when she drew level and steadied her as she tumbled to his side. 'Yuh ain't runnin' clear out to the plains, are yuh?' he said, bringing her deeper into the darkness.

'Hell!' she gulped, coughing on the smoke, blinking on the glare, the flying sparks.

'You said it, gal,' grunted Sam, trying to indicate for a group of wandering townsfolk to stand back. 'Yuh see anythin' of—?' he began.

'Our prowlin' visitor?' croaked Sadie. 'Not close, but I know about him. So does Shard. Yuh got the time to hear?'

'Make it quick.'

Sadie told of what she had heard said about how one-time Marshal John Drew had come to cross the trail of Lucas Shard. 'And I'll tell yuh somethin' for nothin',' she urged, 'if a sonofabitch the likes of Shard's got any respect for anybody, it's John Drew. Biggest shock he's had is findin' him here.'

'And the O'Learys?' asked Sam.

'Ain't sure of their butts from their boots, but if they smell money. . . . Not easy for yuh, but they need corralin' – fast.'

'Ridges?'

'Your guess is as good as mine, Sam, but knowin' him and the way his luck falls—'

They ducked instinctively at a crash of timbers, another shower of sparks and flying splinters.

'Place ain't goin' to stand much longer,' grunted Sam. 'Yuh'd best get back to yuh gals. Get 'em out to the old Simpson barn. Should be safe enough there. Doc's around some place, but as for Henry and Mrs Carfax. . . .'

'What about you?' asked Sadie.

Sam merely grunted again and swung his rifle to a tighter grip in his hands. 'Guess?' he said.

*

'Keep yuh head down, ma'am, f'Crissake – beggin' yuh pardon. No sayin' how itchy them scumbags' fingers are gettin'. Might take to shootin' at anythin' that moves.' Henry Clarke laid a protective hand on Amelia Carfax's shoulder, urging her deeper into the cover behind the counter in his store.

The woman shuddered and bit at her lip. 'The fire, Mr Clarke, it's spreading. There'll be nothing left. We must do something.'

'Not a deal we can do, ma'am, not while we got Shard and them new sidekicks along of him out there. 'Sides, I gotta look to you first. You're my priority 'specially after . . . well, yuh husband dyin' like he did, and the money and that and what happened to you. Heck, ma'am, don't have to spell it out.'

'You don't, Henry, you certainly don't.' The woman's face tightened against the dirt stains and tear streaks. She brushed a straggling of hair to her neck and adjusted her torn, smeared dress as if in preparation for an entrance. 'Whatever Newton was about, it was criminal. I know that now. There's no arguing other. Thankfully, the money is retrieved – for the moment – but there's no saying. . . .' She screwed her eyes at the sizzling crash of timbers at the saloon. 'We have to do something, Henry. Anything's better than more killings, more blood.'

'Them's just what we might be addin' to, ma'am, if we make the wrong move.' Henry crept carefully from the counter, eased to the window and slid behind cover to scan the flame-lit street. 'Sadie and the girls have gotten clear. No sign of Ridges. Nothin' of Sam yet.'

'What about the prowler?' hissed Amelia. 'Is he about? Did he start the fire?'

'Ain't expectin' to see the fella – when have we ever, savin' out there on the plain – but I wouldn't put it past him to have made himself handy with the lucifers. What I ain't figured yet. . . . Hold it. There's Sam.' Henry craned forward. 'Hell, he's closin' in on Shard and his sidekicks. Comin' up on their backs. Damnit, if any one of 'em turns, he'll be dead before he can blink. Why in the name of sanity didn't he get somebody to stand with him? M'self, Casey, Doc – he only had to say. T'ain't no use expectin' them townfolk to lift a finger. Wanderin' about like they were moon-struck. Mebbe I should—'

Henry turned at the click of the store door being opened and the sight of Amelia Carfax slipping into the shadows on the boardwalk.

'Ma'am,' he croaked, coming fully upright. 'No, ma'am, yuh can't, yuh mustn't. Not out there. Hell, they'll gun yuh soon as look at yuh!'

TWENTY-ONE

Only one way for doing this, thought Sam, easing on through the flame-shredded shadows; no point in turning his back on it, hoping something would change the situation as if by magic. Nothing would. Shard and his sidekicks were here, not a hundred yards away, silhouetted like waiting hawks right there in the street, and they had to be stopped before making their next move.

Which is why he was wearing the badge.

He paused at a darkened doorway, took a firmer grip on the rifle, watched as a handful of townsmen scurried to organize against the spread of the fire as the plains' wind freshened, then eased on again, this time veering to the left and a full on view of the three men.

He needed the element of surprise, for the men to be concentrated in their discussion, to be least expecting anyone to raise a hand, much less a gun, against them. Timing, all a question of timing.

Marshal John Drew must have known all about

that, he thought, watching the men. How long before he made a move against Shard? Maybe he was not the only one with a gun trained on the trio. Or was that a straw to clutch at?

He swallowed and slid on.

Scats O'Leary spat into the dirt and shielded his eyes against the glow of the flames. 'So what we waitin' on?' he growled. 'Ain't doin' no good here, are we? Place is lost.'

'It occurred to you, little Brother, to ask yuh dumb self who in hell started this blaze?' frowned Liam. 'Yuh thought that through?'

Scats spat again. 'I figured it. That fella Drew, ain't it? He ain't my problem. Shard here he's trailin'.'

Shard's gaze scanned quickly over the street. 'I ain't for discussin' and arguin'. We do as I say: we get to the livery. If the money's back in town, Sam Berrins is almost certain to have stacked it there. Only place big enough. So that's where we head. Right now, before time runs out on us. Bedrock ain't no place to be.'

'Say that again,' murmured Scats. 'Let's just get to the money and get out. That the way of it, big Brother?'

'Money's what we're here for; money's what we're leavin' with.'

'Glad to hear it,' grinned Scats, idling his fingers over his holstered Colt. 'First sensible thing yuh said in a while. Just a pity about that woman, eh? Shame we couldn't have taken her with us.'

'What the hell yuh wanna go worryin' about a

woman for when there's money—'

The shot ripped across the night like a strangled scream, spinning Liam O'Leary to the ground in a whirl of limbs and a stifled groan.

Shard turned instantly, his Colt drawn and brandished, and headed for the shadows without a second glance at the lifeless Liam.

Scats shouted a curse, dropped to one knee at the body of his brother and released a volley of shots blind and wild into the street.

The menfolk scattered as Sam Berrins stepped into the full glare of the flames, his rifle levelled at Scats.

'Sonofabitch!' screamed the gunslinger. 'Yuh murderin' sonofa goddamn-bitch!'

And then his voice gurgled and bubbled in his throat as if coming to the boil. The Colt fell from his fingers. A stain, dark and crimson spread across his shirt. 'Yuh goddamn-sonofa. . . .' He fell forward, his face burying itself in the dirt and did not move again.

Sam licked quickly at his lips, relaxed, turned slowly, his gaze narrowed, to where he thought the shots had come from.

Henry had left his store, reached the street and stumbled like a drunk into the shadows in search of Amelia Carfax, his curses and calls drowned against the crack of flames, collapse of timbers, shouts and yells of townsmen as they fought to contain the fire and halt its threatened spread to other buildings.

'Of all the darn fool things to go doin',' he moaned as he slid into an alley at the side of the store, staggered into an upturned empty barrel and bruised his shin against a crate.

Hell, he thought, sweating in the heat of the night in spite of the whip of the wind, the woman might have disappeared almost anywhere. Maybe just panicked, upped her skirts and run.

Or maybe not.

Amelia Carfax might be many things, but foolhardy she was not – not the Mrs Carfax he had known all these past years. She would have figured it through, weighed the odds, come to a decision.

So where had she headed? Her home? In search of Lawson Ridges – he, after all, had been in cahoots with her husband, maybe encouraging him – or would she want to keep an eye on that money? She knew where it was stacked.

Henry had hobbled from the alley back to the street, cursing the pain in his shin, and was turning for the livery when Liam O'Leary had hit the dirt like a sack of sodden beans and the night split apart again on the blaze and whine of Winchester fire.

The prowler getting busy, he wondered, stumbling to the nearest cover? Sure as hell sounded like his weapon. He watched from the darkness as Shard took to his heels, saw Scats felled as if no more than tossed aside trash, and peered closer as Sam Berrins turned and scanned the night for the unseen marksman.

'Waste of time, Sam,' he murmured. 'Fella ain't goin' to show and you ain't goin' to find him. Just be grateful he's around and get to Shard before the sonofabitch pulls out.'

He winced and hobbled his way from the deeper darkness, turning again towards the livery. 'What the hell's with this town, anyhow?' grumbled an old-timer falling across Henry's path. 'Tell yuh another thing, place is goin' to be as sober as a preacher 'til they get that saloon fixed. And that ain't no prospect, is it?' The old man staggered away.

Henry blinked as he watched a half-dozen men organize a chain line of water pails to douse the fire, sinking now to a mass of glowing timbers fanned to life here and there by the wind. He blinked again, stiffened and moved on to the livery.

Casey, he knew, would be there, but the place looked deserted.

Sam Berrins hugged the shadows and kept moving, certain that Shard was ahead of him and heading for only one place – the livery. He just hoped Casey was wide awake.

Shard had been equally certain of where he was heading, the livery as tight in his sights as his focus on the money. If the haul was there, it would be his. The fact that he was on his own now was almost a bonus. The only burr in his boot, as ever, was one-time Marshal John Drew. Sheriff Berrins would be no threat.

Making her own way to the livery by the darker route at the rear of the street buildings was an anxious but determined Amelia Carfax.

She had lost a husband and seen her life turned inside out, perhaps ruined, but if there was to be an end to this, then she was going to be there. Shard would be at the livery, she was sure of that. But if he reckoned on it being that easy simply to ride out of Bedrock with the spoils of her husband's stupidity, then he had figured it wrong. The past few days had sharpened her senses, not least for revenge.

But perhaps not put an edge on all her instincts, otherwise she might have noticed the bloodstained, sweat-soaked shape of Lawson Ridges waiting in the shadows only yards ahead of her as she reached the first of the outbuildings at the livery corral.

TWENTY-TWO

'Far enough, Mrs Carfax.' The voice croaked behind the wind like something spawned in a pit of darkness. The woman gasped, her eyes flashing, mouth opening then closing tight as the hand that reached for her settled its slimy, blood-smeared fingers across her lips.

'Hadn't figured for clappin' eyes on you again,' hissed Ridges, dragging Amelia Carfax closer to his side in the pile of timbers, sacking and trash at the back of the outbuilding. 'I should've known better, eh? Ain't for givin' in, are yuh? Like Newton always said, yuh nose'd be the death of yuh. Gettin' close, ain't it?' He eased his fingers on her gasps for breath. 'We're here for the same purpose, I'd say, wouldn't you?'

The woman struggled, spat, then relaxed, conscious of the dazed, fevered look in Ridges' eyes.

'State you're in, mister,' she grimaced, 'you are hardly fit for anything. Best you could do for yourself is—'

'I don't need need advice, lady. Just hold yuh tongue there and do like I say.'

'That being?'

Ridges coughed and wheezed. 'Money's there, in the livery, ain't it? Right. So we need to get our hands on it before that sonofabitch Shard rides out with the better part of it tight in his saddle-bags. How we goin' to do that, lady?'

'I simply wouldn't know,' sniffed the woman. 'But I'm sure you've thought it through.'

'Some. Trouble is, we ain't ironed up. No guns. Problem. Your problem. You could go get a gun – rifle for preference. Try Henry's store, or anywhere back there in the chaos. Yuh bring it here, to me, then, between us we lift the money and clear town. My guarantee you'll be taken good care of soon as I….' He winced on the pain in his leg. 'Soon as I get to a doc.'

'You're crazy,' mocked Amelia. 'Mad. That's the most fool planning I ever heard.'

'Best we got, so we do it. This town don't owe us a thing; yuh husband owes yuh even less, so we take what we can. It's ours. Now, yuh goin' to shift, or stay here 'til yuh choke on widow's weeds?'

Sam Berrins had seen the movement, heard the sound, but there had been no sight of Casey. And why had he doused the lantern?

There had been a passing shadow, thick and heavy, exaggerated by the still firelit night sky where the moon drifted between smoke clouds, but not the shape of the livery owner. Sam flexed his shoulders. Shard – it could only be Shard, already loading up the money with Casey unconscious, or dead, somewhere in a corner.

No waiting now on what had to be done before the scumbag was saddled and loaded up and the money on its way back to the plains' trail.

He licked his lips and narrowed his gaze against the biting wind.

Doc Peppers stumbled across Henry Clarke as the storekeeper had crossed his path in the deepest shadows.

'Shard. Livery. Sam's mebbe there already,' was all he said.

'Got yuh,' Henry grunted. 'Mrs Carfax`s runnin' loose. Watch for her. Yuh seen Ridges?'

'Who cares? Let's move!'

They hurried on like two black hounds pounding across the dirt in the chase for a jack-rabbit supper, the tails of Henry's coat billowing behind him, Doc's hat tight across his eyebrows, neither man aware, it seemed, of the likelihood of Shard stepping out of the night with a levelled Colt all set to blaze.

'Yuh see anythin'?' gasped Henry.

'Not yet. I'm figurin' on Shard bein' a whole lot preoccupied right now. Once we get far side of the corral—'

It was then that the first shots ripped into the night to set the dirt flying and spin Sheriff Sam Berrins flat on his face, his Winchester still blazing even as he fell.

'F'Crissake!' spluttered Henry, diving to the corral for cover. 'That Shard in there? Is Sam hit?'

'Not yet he ain't,' croaked Doc, tumbling to Henry's side. 'But if he stays there much longer. . . .'

The sheriff's rifle blazed again, only to draw another hail of shots from the depths of the livery, kicking dirt in their wild abandon.

'Mebbe we should—' began Henry, then broke into a cold, trickling, stinging sweat. 'Oh, my God,' he moaned, gripping Doc's arm. 'Where the hell did she spring from?'

Doc gulped and broke into his own cold sweat at the sight of Amelia Carfax stumbling across the open space to the corral.

'Get back, ma'am!' yelled Henry, waving his arms. 'Get back! Back!'

But the woman seemed not to hear as she stumbled on, her clothes stained and bedraggled, hair in a blown, matting mass across her shoulders.

Another burst of shots from the livery, this time ripping into the night like flashing blades.

'I'm comin' out,' shouted Shard. 'First one who shoots will be watchin' the woman there bite the dirt. And I ain't kiddin' none. Yuh hear me?'

Amelia Carfax halted, stiff and staring, the wind whipping round her.

Sam struggled to his knees, his rifle slack in his grip. 'We hear yuh. Yuh got my word on it – no shootin'.'

'Hell,' murmured Henry.

'Sonofabitch,' hissed Doc.

'Stay right where yuh are, Mrs Carfax,' said Sam,

his gaze tight on the entrance to the livery. 'That scumbag means exactly what he says. He'll shoot, don't doubt it.' He came slowly, carefully to his feet. 'Yuh got Casey Pike in there, Shard?' he called. 'He still alive?'

'He's alive,' came the answer. 'Sleepin' like a babe this minute. We didn't see eye to eye!'

Sam grunted. Amelia Carfax stood stiff, straight, still staring. Henry Clarke swallowed on a dirt-scuffed throat. Doc sweated. The wind whipped, moaned, lifted the dust and nagged at loose brush.

It was Henry's hand that reached for Doc's arm ahead of a croak and a nod of his head to the left. 'See there,' he whispered. 'Would yuh look at that?'

Doc said nothing as he turned his grey, tired gaze to the open ground to the street and the shape that moved steadily forward against the flame-glazed night sky and the haunted silhouette of Bedrock.

'John Drew,' murmured Sam, watching the approach of the shape, then switching his gaze anxiously to the livery and the bulk of Lucas Shard mounted on a horse heavy with packed saddle-bags.

Shard reined back, waited a moment. 'That who I think it is?' he called, his eyes burning, lips twisted on a slanted, sweating grin. 'That you, Drew? I figured so. Knew you'd catch up sooner or later. Sooner suits me right now.' He spat deep into the dirt. 'Kinda busy, as yuh can see. Places to go, so we'll make this brief, eh? Get it done. I ain't one for holdin' a grudge that long. And, frankly, you're becomin' a real pain in the butt.'

John Drew halted, legs apart to balance his hold

on the Winchester drawn across his body.

'Hear yuh've been havin' quite a time here,' drawled Shard. 'Makin' a real name for yourself.' The grin began to flatten. 'Well, I'm sure the good folk of Bedrock won't wanna see yuh go, so how about we arrange a permanent place for yuh here. Somethin' real tasteful – top of Boot Hill!'

Shard's first shot from his mounted position forced his horse to buck to the left; his second set the animal turning through a half-circle, and he was into his third when Drew's Winchester spat viciously into life, once, twice, then through a ranging volley that threw Shard from his mount and left him crawling, clawing helplessly for his weapon stranded yards from his reach.

The Winchester spat again as Shard raised his head for the last time, his stare already emptying to the sockets of a skull as the lead ripped the life from his body and spread the blood in a seeping stain.

Then only the plains' wind wept on the silence and the wolf was gone.

TWENTY-THREE

He looked affluent, a man of some wealth and property; well dressed in tailored Eastern-style clothes; a man more at home in the city than the dust and dirt of Bedrock.

But he was here, and with good reason, thought Sam Berrins, leaning back in his chair at his desk, watching carefully as Jasper McCulligan, president of the West-Pacific Railroad Company, consulted his timepiece, grunted, clicked the piece shut and crossed the office to the dust-streaked window.

'Fact is, Sheriff,' he said, turning slowly to Sam, his thumbs hooked in the cut of his fancy-patterned waistcoat, 'the one-time marshal, John Drew, is his own man, always has been, no changing him neither, and certainly not since the loss of his wife in such tragic circumstances.' He coughed lightly, clearing his throat. 'Yes, well ... maybe all that is now resolved. Lucas Shard is dead, and he died at the hand, in my view, of his rightful executioner.'

It was Sam Berrins's turn to grunt and glance quickly at Doc Peppers, Henry Clarke and Casey Pike seated at his side. 'Ain't nobody arguin' with that,' he said. 'But what we still ain't figured—'

'A moment if you please,' gestured McCulligan, raising an arm. 'You say you have seen nothing of Drew since the night of the fire and the shooting? Just so, and nor will you. Most I've had is this.' He drew a folded, single sheet of paper from an inside pocket. 'A simple, straightforward, no-frills explanation of what happened here. I had not expected more. And this, gentlemen, is certainly more than you are likely to get.'

'So he was working for you and your company?' said Doc.

'Not in our direct employ, but retained by us to look into areas of, shall we say, a doubtful nature. This was one such case.'

'How come?' asked Henry, leaning forward.

McCulligan's thumbs went back to his waistcoat. 'Carfax's sale of the rail bonds – against shareholders' wishes – had been known to us for some time. What we planned was to catch him red-handed with the money and whoever was working along of him. John Drew took on the job and stayed all the way with it once he discovered Shard had been recruited as the leading gunslinger in the planned escape with Ridges to the border, though you can be certain Ridges would have perished along with all the others when the time came. Carfax was no gentleman.'

'Tell that to his widow!' grimaced Casey.

'Well, Drew sure played one helluva game with us,' said Sam. 'All that prowlin' around, leavin' notes. . . . Heck, he might've said somethin'.'

'And risk not bringing the likes of Dyke, Mabbutt, Connors, the O'Learys to book? Missing out on a showdown with Shard? I think not,' said McCulligan. 'No, Bedrock was to be the place, the time, and that's how it happened. Territory's a whole lot cleaner for the flushing.'

'That's true,' murmured Sam, 'in spite of the state of the town, the mess, the losses. . . .'

'Shareholders' money's been recovered in full,' smiled McCulligan. 'You're all in for a generous reward. How yuh goin' to spend it?'

They built a new saloon and renamed it The Silver Key, with Sadie Shaw and Amelia Carfax in partnership as the proprietors. 'Best welcome anywheres across the Seroquoi plains – especially the ladies!' was the proud testimony handed down that drew a steady stream of travellers heading West.

Henry Clarke expanded his store; Casey, the livery, as the town lay its claim to fame as the place where Lucas Shard had finally bit on the dirt and the O'Learys died in the showdown with John Drew.

Doc Peppers patched Larsen Ridges best he could and Sam granted him freedom till he cleared the plains. After that, he was on his own. He was never heard of again.

Doc settled in his eventual retirement to writing the official account of the events of that fall and the coming to Bedrock of Marshal John Drew.

Sheriff Sam Berrins continues to wear the badge of the law and to watch over what he describes as a 'tight, tidy town'. Some say as how he holds Amelia

Carfax in high regard and that one day they might get to being wed.

Meantime, come the late summer winds off the Seroquoi plains, Sam can be seen riding the perimeters of the town as if expecting to see John Drew clear the distant horizon on his long-awaited return to Bedrock. But most reckon that will never come to pass, and in any case, the plains' winds these days are not for arriving so early. Strange thing is, though, a lone wolf has set to howling out there long after dark.

But nobody has ever seen it. Yet.